美國孩子 天天用的
英文文法

Aman Chiu 著

新雅文化事業有限公司
www.sunya.com.hk

學好英文文法，從聽說讀寫入手！

Grammar items 文法知識

本書分為 15 個單元，包含 100 個小學階段必須掌握的英文文法知識，涵蓋單詞和句子，內容豐富又齊全！

Let's listen

透過聆聽簡單的生活對話，認識文法的基礎概念。

Let's learn

透過閱讀簡潔的教學文字和例子，重點理解文法知識。

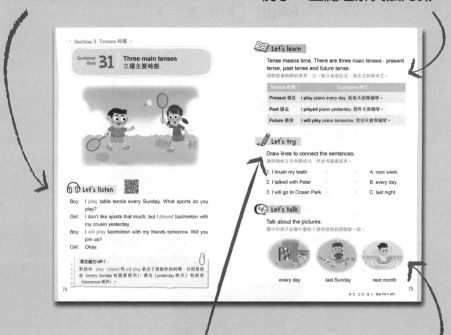

Let's try

動腦又動筆，完成應用文法知識的題目，鞏固所學。

Let's talk

在對話中實踐，說出文法正確的句子。

配備各種輔助工具，助你輕鬆學習！

二維碼 QR Code

只要使用智能手機或平板電腦等設備，在連接網絡的狀態下掃描二維碼（QR Code），便可收聽美國孩子說出融入了文法知識的生活對話！

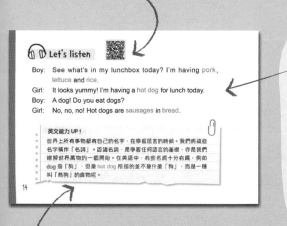

網上中文版

聆聽 Let's listen 中的對話時，可掃描下面的二維碼（QR Code），在網上查看中文翻譯內容，幫助理解！

掃一掃！
中英對照版

英文能力 UP!

解讀文法中的常犯錯誤或特殊用法，提升英文的運用能力！

小提示

提供額外的文法知識，助你回答題目！

跟美國孩子天天快樂學文法！

詳細附錄表格，容易查閱！

設不規則動詞表，包含小學階段常用的 135 個不規則動詞！

以遊戲檢測學習成果，樂在其中！

本書設 5 個 Let's play 小遊戲，在學習相關的文法知識後使用，輕鬆檢測學習成果！

文法手帳隨身帶，隨時隨地練文法！

隨書附送 6 張「文法手帳」雙面印刷卡，把 12 個英文文法要點歸納整理成簡單清楚的表格，更搭配圖片幫助理解。孩子可以把它剪下來隨身攜帶，方便學習！

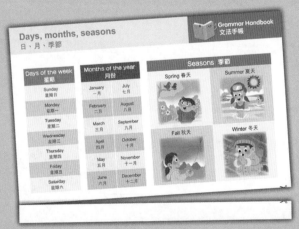

剪下來！

文法該如何學？如何能學好它？

對於很多孩子來說，學習英文文法相當困難，坊間許多教授文法的書重點都在講解文法規則，然後不斷重複練習。這種形式把文法割裂開來，作為單一重點施教，結果變成一種強力灌輸的教學模式，要求孩子死記硬背。這對他們來說相當枯燥乏味，甚至會造成壓力，產生逃避的心態。

文法該如何學？如何能學好它？甚至究竟要不要學文法？這些問題在腦海裏盤旋多年。也許是這個緣故，一直以來都想為廣大兒童編寫一本能真正切合他們需要的文法參考書，目的是要讓孩子在打下扎實語文根基的同時，能夠輕鬆愉快地學習英語。設計這本書的第一個前提是「生活」——文法來自語言，語言來自生活。如能把文法還原於生活，從生活中認識文法、掌握文法，就能使它變得鮮活起來。

第二個前提是把文法學習整合在「聽說讀寫」四大技能的訓練裏。語言是一個整體，不能完全割裂。這四種技能緊密關聯，相互影響，其中聽說是一對矛盾，訓練聽力即訓練口語，反之亦然；讀寫是另一對矛盾，兩者亦不可分家。每篇課文的設計從聆聽開始（**Let's listen**），「先聽說、後讀寫」是學習任何語言的理想手段，我嘗試把每個文法重點融入簡單的生活對話中，孩子可以反覆聆聽，從生活入手認識文法的基礎概念。

其次是 **Let's learn**，這部分以最簡單的文字連同適量的例子，把文法知識整理出來，重點是閱讀和理解。理解文法概念後，便進入寫的訓練了（**Let's try**）。這部分要求孩子動腦動筆，鞏固所學。課文最後以 **Let's talk** 作結，把說話訓練結合在互動遊戲中，重新把文法拉回生活當中，形成一個循環。

本書包含了小學階段必須掌握的 **100** 個文法重點，從單詞開始，到句子組成為終結。每課濃縮在一個對頁內，讓各個重點變得簡潔，又容易掌握。學習文法必須是基礎與樂趣並重，讓孩子在愉快的氣氛下學好英語，不緊不慢地打好基礎。

Aman Chiu

Contents 目錄

Section 6

Adjectives 形容詞

Section 7 Modals 情態動詞

Section 14　Passive Voice and Indirect Speech 被動語態和間接敘述

Section 15　Sentences 句子

| Grammar item 1 | **Common nouns - Things**
普通名詞：事物 |

 Let's listen

Boy: See what's in my lunchbox today? I'm having pork, lettuce and rice.

Girl: It looks yummy! I'm having a hot dog for lunch today.

Boy: A dog! Do you eat dogs?

Girl: No, no, no! Hot dogs are sausages in bread.

英文能力 UP！

世界上所有事物都有自己的名字，在學習語言的時候，我們將這些名字稱作「名詞」。認識名詞，是學習任何語言的基礎，亦是我們瞭解世界萬物的一個開始。在英語中，有些名詞十分有趣，例如 dog 指「狗」，但是 hot dog 所指的並不是什麼「狗」，而是一種叫「熱狗」的食物呢。

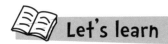

Let's learn

Everything has a name. A noun is the name of a thing.

所有事物都有一個名稱，名詞就是用來表達各種事物的名稱。

Examples 例子		
pork 豬肉	lettuce 生菜	rice 米飯
pizza 薄餅	carrot 蘿蔔	tomato 番茄
ice cream 雪糕	apple 蘋果	fish 魚

Let's try

What's in this lunchbox? Name the food.

這個飯盒裏有什麼呢？請在橫線上填上適當的食物名詞。

1. _____

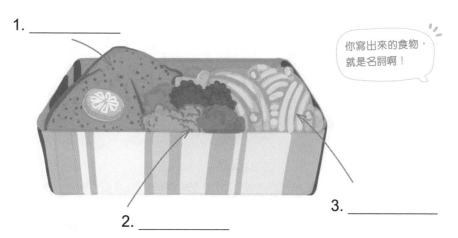

你寫出來的食物，就是名詞啊！

2. _____

3. _____

Let's talk

What are you having for lunch today? Talk about them.

你今天午餐吃什麼呢？請説一説。

I'm having _____ for lunch today.

Let's try 答案：1. drumstick 2. vegetables 3. noodles

> **Grammar item 2** | **Common nouns - People**
> 普通名詞：人物

 Let's listen

Boy: What's your mother's job?

Girl My mother is a teacher. She teaches in a primary school. What's yours?

Boy: My mother is a housewife. She stays at home, does housework and takes care of us. And she is a great cooker.

Girl: Are you kidding me? Your mom can't be a cooker!

英文能力 UP！

有些職業名稱是從動詞加詞尾 -er 衍生出來，例如 sing + er 就是 singer（歌手），但是 cook + er 並不是指「廚師」，而是「飯鍋」或「煮食爐」呢！如果想表達煮食的人，應用 cook，例如 She is a good cook.（她是個好廚師。）

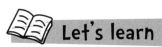
Let's learn

Nouns are the names for everyday people.

名詞會用來指日常生活中遇見的人,當中包括人的身分和職業。

Identity 人的身分	boy 男孩	girl 女孩	cousin 表兄弟姐妹
	mother 母親	father 父親	grandmother (外)祖母
Jobs 職業	athlete 運動員	hairdresser 理髮師	doctor 醫生
	musician 音樂家	scientist 科學家	writer 作家

Let's try

Guess the jobs.

請在橫線上填上適當的職業名詞。

> 在家裏,你是 son or daughter(兒子 / 女兒),也許還是 brother or sister(兄弟 / 姐妹)。在學校裏,你則是 pupil(學生)。

1. My father is a _____.
   He puts out fires.

2. My mother is a _____. She takes care of sick people.

3. My uncle is a _____. He drives buses.

Let's talk

What do you want to be when you grow up? Talk about it.

你長大以後想做什麼工作呢?請說一說。

> I want to be a / an _____.

Let's try 答案:1. fireman 2. nurse 3. driver

Grammar item **3** | **Common nouns - Animals and plants**
普通名詞：動植物

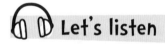 **Let's listen**

Girl: There's an owl in the tree. Can you see it?

Boy: I can't see it. It's too dark. But I can see a very big cat behind the bushes!

Girl: That's not a cat. It's a leopard! And behind the leopard there's a lion!

Boy: Oh, no! I'm scared!

英文能力 UP！

地球上的動物、植物、昆蟲數以萬計，牠/它們各有自己的名稱。
例如 owl（貓頭鷹）、cat（貓）、leopard（豹）、lion（獅子）便是動物的名稱，tree（樹）、bushes（灌木叢）則是植物的名稱。

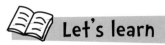 **Let's learn**

Nouns are also the names for animals, plants, insects, etc.

名詞也可指動物、植物、昆蟲等。

	Examples 例子		
Animals 動物	chicken 雞	duck 鴨子	horse 馬
	crocodile 鱷魚	crab 螃蟹	panda 熊貓
Plants 植物	grass 草	flower 花	rose 玫瑰
Insects 昆蟲	ant 螞蟻	bee 蜜蜂	fly 蒼蠅

 **Let's try**

Guess the animals.

請在橫線上填上適當的動物名詞。

1. I have wings but I'm not a bird. I used to be a caterpillar.

   I'm a _____.

2. I live in lakes and rivers. I have four legs and a long tail.

   I have lots of sharp teeth. I'm a _____.

 Let's talk

What is your favorite animal? Talk about it.

你最喜歡的動物是什麼呢？請説一説。

My favorite animal is the _____.

<table>
<tr><td>Grammar
item</td><td>**4**</td><td>**Common nouns - Gender**
普通名詞：不同性別的名詞</td></tr>
</table>

 Let's listen

Boy: Look! The lion is feeding her cubs. They look so happy.

Girl: That's not a lion. It's a lioness.

Boy: A lioness?

Girl: Yes. A lioness is a female lion. She has no (mane.) 鬃毛 Male lions do not look after the cubs, but they do protect the family from other fierce animals.

英文能力 UP！

在談及人或動物時，英文名詞一般不會區分男性（雄性）或女性（雌性），但也有部分名詞會經由不同的單詞來表示性別，例如 lion（雄獅）和 lioness（母獅）。

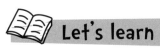

Let's learn

Some names of people or animals have different names to refer to male or female.

有些人物或動物名稱會使用不同的單詞，來表示男女或雌雄兩種不同的性別。

People 人物		Animals 動物	
Male 男性	Female 女性	Male 雄性	Female 雌性
man 男人	woman 女人	rooster 公雞	hen 母雞
prince 王子	princess 公主	tiger 老虎	tigress 雌虎
policeman 男警員	policewoman 女警員	billy goat 公山羊	nanny goat 母山羊

Let's try

Draw lines to pair up the words.

請配對以下名詞，然後用線連起來。

1. husband ·   · A. waitress

2. emperor ·   · B. empress

3. waiter ·   · C. wife

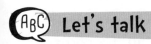

Let's talk

Can you tell the names of the opposite gender for these words?

這些名詞的另一個性別是什麼？請說一說。

✿ king   ✿ grandmother   ✿ goddess

Grammar item **5** | **Common nouns - Places**
普通名詞：地方

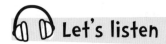 Let's listen

Boy: I heard there's a place where there's no work but all play.

Girl: Really? I doubt it.

Boy: I found this very strange map in the library. It says "Go down the street, take a right at the post office. When you get to a church, take a left. It's right round the corner from a museum over there."

Girl: That sounds a little weird. I think it's a prank.

惡作劇

英文能力 UP！

正如世界上每種事物都有名字，地球上每個地方當然也有各自的名稱，包括大自然的山河大地，或人們建設的社區場所，例如 library（圖書館）、street（街道）、church（教堂）、post office（郵政局）、museum（博物館）等。

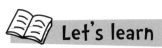

Let's learn

Nouns are also the names for places.

名詞也可用來指地方。

	Examples 例子		
Nature 大自然	beach 海灘	lake 湖泊	forest 森林
	seashore 海邊	mountain 山	ocean 海洋
Community 社區	school 學校	library 圖書館	market 菜市場
	supermarket 超級市場	playground 遊樂場	hospital 醫院

Let's try

Circle the places in the sentences.

請把句中代表地方的名詞圈出來。

1. We are going to the museum.

2. Camels live in deserts.

3. Dad works in a bank.

> 可以用「go to + 地方名詞」來表示「去某個地方」，例如 go to the supermarket / zoo（去超級市場／動物園）等；go home（回家）則是例外。

 # Let's talk

Talk about the places near where you live. Make as many sentences as you can.

你家附近有哪些場所呢？請説一説，並多列舉幾個例子。

> There is a _____ (e.g. *park*) near my home.

Grammar item **6** | **Proper nouns**
專有名詞

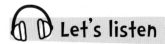 **Let's listen**

Girl: Lily is going to Japan at Christmas. She is going to visit the Wizarding World of Harry Potter.

Boy: Wow, I would love to go there one day!

Girl: But Lily's not very happy about it. She can't take Roger with her. She doesn't want to leave Roger alone.

Boy: Roger? Do you mean her doggie?

英文能力 UP！

普通名詞泛指某些人或事物，而專有名詞指的是特定的人或事物，例如 Lily（人物）、Japan（地方）、Christmas（節日）、Wizarding World of Harry Potter（地方）、Roger（動物）。

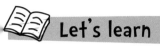 **Let's learn**

When we give a special name to a thing, person, animal or place, it is a proper noun.

專有名詞是特定的人物、地方或獨一無二的事物的名稱。

	Examples 例子		
Dates 特定的日期	Monday 星期一	January 一月	Christmas 聖誕節
People 人物	Mr. Smith 史密夫先生	Harry Potter 哈利波特	Snow White 白雪公主
Nationality or language 種族或語言	Chinese 中國人；中文	Asian 亞洲人	English 英國人；英文
Places 地方	Hong Kong 香港	Ocean Park 海洋公園	Mount Fuji 富士山

 **Let's try**

Correct the sentences.

請改正句子，然後填在橫線上。

> 記住專有名詞的第一個字母要大寫。

1. anna's birthday is in july.

_____

2. Aunt judy can speak japanese.

_____

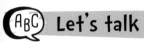 **Let's talk**

Talk about yourself.

請用以下句式介紹自己。

My name is _____. I was born in _____.

| Grammar item | **7** | **Collective nouns** 集合名詞 |

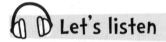 Let's listen

Boy: Bwahhhahahaaa!

Girl: What's so funny?

Boy: This is a very funny book. A herd of elephants was bathing in the river. Then, a swarm of bees attacked the elephants. The elephants splashed water at the bees and the bees turned to attack a flock of sheep.

Girl: And then?

英文能力 UP！

對話中的動物（elephants, bees and sheep）是一羣一羣地出現的，這個時候我們就需要使用集合名詞來描述牠們了！

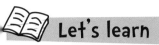

Let's learn

A collective noun is the name for a group of people, animals or things.

好幾個人物、動物或物件聚集起來，就成為一個集合名詞。

	Examples 例子	
People 人物	a **family** 一個家庭	a **class** 一個班級
	a **team** 一個隊伍	a **choir** 一個合唱團
Animals 動物	a **flock** of sheep 一羣綿羊	a **swarm** of bees 一羣蜜蜂
	a **herd** of elephants 一羣大象	a **school** of fish 一羣魚
Things 物件	a **bunch** of grapes 一串葡萄	a **bouquet** of flowers 一束花
	a **pack** of cards 一副紙牌	a **set** of dishes 一套碗碟

Let's try

Draw lines to pair up the words.

請配對以下單詞，然後用線連起來。

1. a bunch of　　　　·　　　　　　·　　A. pupils

2. a class of　　　　·　　　　　　·　　B. bananas

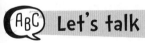

Let's talk

Tell a story with these two pictures.

請發揮創意和想像力，利用以下兩幅圖說說故事。

a crowd of people

a pack of dogs

Let's try 答案：1. B　2. A

Grammar item **8** | **Singular and plural nouns**
單數與複數名詞

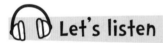 Let's listen

Girl: Let me sing you a song. One little, two little, three little fingers. Four little, five little, six little fingers. Seven little, eight little, nine little fingers. Ten little fingers here.

Boy: Haha, that's funny. Let me sing you a song too. One little, two little, three little dinosaurs. Four little, five little, six little dinosaurs. Seven little, eight little, nine little dinosaurs. Ten little dinosaurs.

英文能力 UP！

英語中的普通名詞分為可數與不可數兩種。使用可數名詞時，可在前面加上 a 或 an，或用複數形式，例如 a finger（一隻手指）、ten fingers（十隻手指）、one dinosaur（一隻恐龍）、ten dinosaurs（十隻恐龍）。

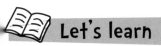 **Let's learn**

Singular countable nouns refer to one person or thing. Plural countable nouns refer to more than one person or thing. The plural form is generally formed by adding **-s** to the singular.

單數可數名詞指一個人或一種事物，複數可數名詞指多於一個人或一種事物。一般來說，我們會在名詞後加 -s 來表示複數。

Singular 單數	Plural 複數
a dog 一隻狗 →	two dog**s** 兩隻狗
the boy 那個男孩 →	some boy**s** 一些男孩
that book 那本書 →	those book**s** 那些書
my T-shirt 我的 T 恤 →	many T-shirt**s** 很多 T 恤
注意：一般與 a / an、the、that、my 等連用。	注意：如果名詞是可數的，就可以用表示數量的單詞，例如 a few、some、many。

 **Let's try**

Fill in the blanks with the correct plural nouns.

請在橫線填上正確的複數名詞。

1. One duckling, a few _____.

2. One river, some _____.

 Let's talk

How many clothing items do you have? Talk about it.

看看你的衣櫃，裏面有多少衣物呢？請說一說。

I have _____ (e.g. *six T-shirts*).

Let's try 答案：1. ducklings 2. rivers

Grammar item 9 | **Plural countable nouns**
複數可數名詞

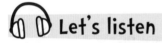 **Let's listen**

Boy: What're those tiny little creatures the cat is chasing after?

Girl: Are they fireflies? Or moths? Or butterflies?

Boy: No, they look nothing like a firefly or a butterfly but a human with wings.

Girl: Oh, they're fairies! They're just so cute. I wish I were a fairy, too.

英文能力 UP！

除了加 -s 來表示外，複數可數名詞還有其他不同的形式，例如 firefly（螢火蟲）的複數是 fireflies、butterfly（蝴蝶）的複數是 butterflies、fairy（小仙子）的複數是 fairies，可不能直接加 -s 啊！

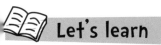

Let's learn

Follow these rules to form the plurals.

把可數名詞從單數變為複數，有以下一些規則。

Rules 規則	Singular 單數	Plural 複數
以 -s、-sh、-ch、-x、-z 或 -o 結尾的名詞，後方應加上 -es	watch 手錶	watches
	tomato 番茄	tomatoes
以 -y 結尾的名詞，先把 y 改成 i，再加上 -es	baby 嬰兒	babies
	ferry 渡輪	ferries
以 -f 或 -fe 結尾的名詞，先把 f、fe 改成 v，再加上 -es	wolf 狼	wolves
	knife 刀	knives

Let's try

Fill in the blanks with the correct plural nouns.

請在橫線上填上複數名詞的正確形式。

1. Let's make three _____ (wish).

2. The police have caught the _____ (thief).

ABC Let's talk

Count and talk about them.

數一數，然後説出來。

1.

2.

3.

Grammar item **10** | **Irregular plural nouns**
不規則複數名詞

 Let's listen

Boy: I think I just saw a mouse running out of the kitchen.

Girl: I saw something running across the living room floor last night.

Boy: Oh no! How do these mice get into your house? These cookies look like something has chewed on them.

Girl: We might have eaten the cookies that mice had chewed on! I am absolutely terrified! I'll tell mom about this.

英文能力 UP！

有些複數名詞變化是完全沒有規律的，例如 mouse（老鼠）的複數是 mice。此外，有些名詞的單數和複數可以是相同的，例如 sheep（羊）的複數同樣是 sheep。

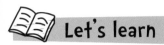

Let's learn

Some common nouns have irregular plurals.

有些複數名詞會出現不規則的變化。

Singular 單數	Plural 複數	Singular 單數	Plural 複數
man 男人	men	foot 腳	feet
woman 女人	women	goose 鵝	geese
child 小孩	children	tooth 牙齒	teeth
person 人	people	cattle 牛	cattle

Let's try

Write the plural form of each noun.

請在橫線上填上正確的複數名詞。

> 只要多看，就能好好記住這類複數名詞了。

1. Ducks, swans and _____ (goose) are birds.

2. _____ (deer), sheep and mice are mammals.

3. Sharks, _____ (tuna) and mackerel are fish.

Let's talk

Read this tongue twister aloud.

請大聲朗讀這個繞口令吧。

Out of the three deer

and six sheep,

Cheer is a deer that

thinks he's a sheep.

Grammar item **11** | Uncountable nouns 不可數名詞

 Let's listen

Girl: Mom says the most important meal of the day is breakfast.

Boy: Yeah, but I don't usually have time to eat a big breakfast. I usually just have a bowl of cereal. That's it. What do you want to eat for breakfast today?

Girl: I will have oatmeal, some toast and orange juice. I like lots of jam on my toast. That is what I usually have.

英文能力 UP！

我們早餐吃的食物有許多都是不可數名詞，意思是不能直接數算它們的數量，因此不能在前面加上 a 或 an，或在後面加 -s 或 -es。如要表示這些食物的數量，就得用 some、a lot of、lots of、much、a bit of、a great deal of 這類表示多少的量詞來表達。

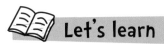 **Let's learn**

An uncountable noun is something we don't count. It has no plural.

不可數名詞無法用數字來計算，它可能是抽象的概念、沒有實質的形態或體積太小。這類名詞通常沒有複數形式，可用單數形式來表示。

	Examples 例子	
Liquid 液體	juice 果汁	milk 牛奶
Gas 氣體	air 空氣	smoke 煙
Food 食物	bread 麵包	sugar 糖
Nature 大自然	thunder 雷	sunshine 陽光
Materials or others 物料及其他	paper 紙張	furniture 家具

 **Let's try**

Circle the uncountable nouns in the sentences.

請把句中的不可數名詞圈出來。

1. She is drinking a cup of tea.

2. The table is covered with dust.

(ABC) Let's talk

Name a food or drink that can be put into the following containers. Use uncountable nouns. Talk about them.

有什麼食物或飲料可以放進以下容器？請用不可數名詞説一説。

a glass of _____

a teaspoon of _____

Let's try 答案：1. tea 2. dust

Grammar item	**12**	**Abstract nouns** 抽象名詞

 Let's listen

Boy: What's wrong? Why do you look so scared?

Girl: There is something standing in the corner over there.

Boy: What's that? I can't see anything.

Girl: It's a ghost! I saw a ghost! It just stood there just now. It didn't really have a face or anything, just a long shadowy thing that I couldn't figure out what it was.

幽暗、模糊

英文能力 UP！

抽象名詞與一般名詞不同之處，就是抽象名詞不是實物，而且大多沒有明顯的外觀，例如對話中的 ghost（鬼魂）便是看不清、摸不到，虛無縹緲，抽象極了！

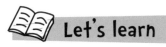 **Let's learn**

Sometimes, a noun is something we cannot really see or touch. They are words for ideas, feelings, or experiences. We call these nouns abstract nouns.

抽象名詞是指那些看不見、摸不著，只能憑想像或經驗來理解的概念。

Examples 例子			
childhood 童年	illness 疾病	courage 勇氣	joy 歡樂
friendship 友誼	time 時間	beauty 美	knowledge 學問
peace 和平	laziness 懶惰	honesty 誠實	strength 力量

 Let's try

Circle the abstract nouns in the sentences.

請把句中的抽象名詞圈出來。

> 抽象名詞大多是不可數名詞，但也有例外，例如剛才提及的 ghost。

1. Everybody loves freedom.

2. Is there any hope that we will win?

3. Fruit and vegetables are good for your health.

 Let's talk

Act out these words using gestures alone. Ask your parents to guess.

請利用表情和動作扮演以下名詞表達的意思，讓你父母猜一猜吧。

 anger   fear   love

 Guess what I am acting out?

Let's try 答案：1. freedom   2. hope   3. health

37

Grammar item 13 | Indefinite articles - a / an (1)
不定冠詞（1）

 Let's listen

Boy: What's that strange shadow in the water?

Girl: It looks really big. Is it an otter or a seal?

Boy: No, it's not an otter or a seal. It has arms – eight long arms! It's an octopus!

Girl: It's a giant octopus! Wow, look! It's chasing after a dolphin and a ray! It wants to eat them!

英文能力 UP！

中文的「一隻」和「一條」變成英文後統統用 a / an，例如 a seal（一隻海豹）、an otter（一隻水獺）、an octopus（一隻八爪魚）、a dolphin（一條海豚）和 a ray（一條魔鬼魚）。

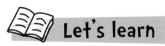 **Let's learn**

Indefinite articles are *a* and *an*. They mean 'one', referring to a single object or person.

不定冠詞有兩個：a 和 an。如果名詞的數量只有一個，我們就會把它放在名詞前面。

Rules 規則	Examples 例子	
Consonant 以子音開首	a school 一所學校	a pencil 一枝鉛筆
	a house 一間房子	a window 一扇窗
Vowel 以元音開首（即 a, e, i, o, u）	an axe 一把斧頭	an egg 一顆雞蛋
	an elephant 一隻大象	an iron 一個熨斗
	an orange 一個橙	an umbrella 一把雨傘

 **Let's try**

Draw lines to group the words.

請選出以下名詞需要哪個冠詞，然後用線連起來。

a　　**an**

boy　　ant　　owl　　ear

Let's talk

Draw the words and talk about them.

請畫一畫以下詞語，然後說一說你畫了什麼。

a book	an ice cream	a fish

Grammar item **14** | ### Indefinite articles - a / an (2)
不定冠詞（2）

 Let's listen

Boy: I saw a UFO last night.

Girl: Where did you see it?

Boy: In the park. A unicorn came out of it. I was afraid at first, but then I realized he was very friendly. We talked for an hour. He even invited me to go for a ride in his UFO.

Girl: Are you kidding me? Was it a dream?

英文能力 UP！

區別 a 和 an 的用法時，不僅看字首的字母，還要注意發音。有的
單詞字首是子音字母，但實際卻是發元音，例如 an hour（一個小
時）。相反有些單詞字首是元音字母，但實際是發子音，例如 a
unicorn（一隻獨角獸）。

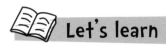 **Let's learn**

We use *a* before a word that starts in **u** or **eu** when it sounds like 'you'. We use *an* before a word that starts with a silent **h**.

以 u 或 eu 字母開頭，讀起來像「you」的單詞前要用 a。而以 h 字母開頭，但 h 不發音的單詞前要用 an。

Rules 規則	Examples 例子	
Sounds like 'you' 讀音像「you」	a unicorn 一隻獨角獸	a uniform 一套制服
	a European 一個歐洲人	a university 一所大學
Silent h h 不發音	an hour 一個小時	an honest boy 一個誠實的男孩
注意：以元音開首的縮寫詞同樣跟以上規則	a UFO 一架飛碟	a USA citizen 一個美國市民

 **Let's try**

Circle the correct answers.

請把正確的冠詞圈出來。

1. They returned after (a / an) hour.

2. Tom is (a / an) European. He is (a / an) Italian.

(ABC) Let's talk

Read this tongue twister aloud.

請大聲朗讀這個繞口令吧。

A unicorn wearing a uniform is flying a UFO.

Grammar item **15** | Definite article - the (1) 定冠詞（1）

 Let's listen

Boy: I saw a film last Sunday.

Girl: What was the film about?

Boy: It was about an alien and a boy. They made friends with each other and then the alien took the boy to Mars. He'd certainly never seen anything like that before. Then, the boy met a girl.

Girl: Was the girl an alien too? Was she friendly too?

英文能力 UP！

對話中的一組組單詞有先後次序：先用 a 或 an，然後再用 the。那 用來表示起初不知道指的是什麼事，後來已經知道了，意思就好像 中文的「這個」、「那個」。

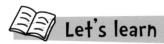 **Let's learn**

We use *a* or *an* for the person or thing you mention the first time, then we use *the* when you mention that person or thing again.

我們第一次提及某人或物件時，會把 a 或 an 放在那個名詞前面。當我們再次提起該人或物件，便要改用 the。

Mention the first time 第一次提及	Mention again 再次提起
I bought **a book**. 我買了一本書。	**The book** was about animals. 那是一本關於動物的書。
I saw **an alien**. 我見到一個外星人。	**The alien** could talk. 那個外星人會說話。
I had **a hamburger** for lunch. 我的午餐是漢堡包。	**The hamburger** was delicious. 那個漢堡包很好吃。

 Let's try

Fill in the blanks with the correct articles.

請在橫線上填上正確的冠詞。

1. I had _____ ice cream for dessert. I liked _____ ice cream a lot.

2. She bought _____ new school bag. _____ school bag is yellow in color.

3. They live in _____ old house. There is a lake behind _____ house.

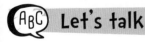 **Let's talk**

What book have you read recently? Talk about it.

你最近閱讀了哪本書呢？請說一說。

> I read a book. The book was about _____.

Grammar item **16** | **Definite article - the (2)**
定冠詞（2）

 Let's listen

Girl: The sky has turned very dark. I feel scared.

Boy: How round and bright the moon is tonight! I've heard that a full moon can turn people into werewolves!

Girl: Oh no! I'm afraid of werewolves! They kill people for food. They need blood to survive. I'm totally frightened of being eaten by those scary monsters.

Boy: Come on! Werewolves don't really exist in the world.

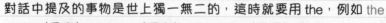

英文能力 UP！

對話中提及的事物是世上獨一無二的，這時就要用 the，例如 the moon（月亮）、the sky（天空）、the world（世界）等。

44

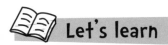 **Let's learn**

We use *the* when we are speaking of one particular person, place or thing.

如果指的人物、地方或事物是唯一的，我們就會用定冠詞 the。

	Examples 例子		
Person 人物	**the** Principal 校長	**the** President 總統	**the** Queen 皇后
Place 地方	**the** Peak 山頂	**the** countryside 郊外	**the** park 公園
	the Pacific Ocean 太平洋	**the** North Pole 北極	**the** equator 赤道
Thing 事物	**the** earth 地球	**the** moon 月球	**the** sky 天空
	the government 政府	**the** east / west 東方 / 西方	**the** past / future 過去 / 未來

 **Let's try**

Insert articles where necessary.

請在句中適當的地方加上冠詞。

1. Beijing is capital of China.

2. How blue sky looks!

3. We should protect earth.

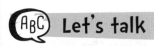 **Let's talk**

Read this tongue twister aloud.

請大聲朗讀這個繞口令吧。

The children eat the chicken in the kitchen.

Let's try 答案：1. Beijing is the capital of China. 2. How blue the sky looks! 3. We should protect the earth.

45

Grammar item **17** | **Zero articles** 零冠詞

 Let's listen

Girl: There's a dog over there. It's so cute. Hey, come here, doggie!

Boy: Careful!

Girl: Why are you so nervous? Dogs are friendly and they won't bite.

Boy: I don't think so. I'm afraid of dogs. I was once bitten by a dog when I was still a little boy, and now that's the only memory of dogs I have.

英文能力 UP！

這裏的 dogs 並不是指許多隻狗，而是泛指狗這個類別。因此，我們不用加上任何冠詞，例如不會説 I'm afraid of a dog / the dog.

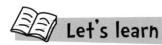 **Let's learn**

We don't use *the* before a noun when we mean something in general. We say *the* when we mean something in particular.

敘述某類事物時不在名詞前面加冠詞,即「零冠詞」。提及特定的事物時,我們才用 the。

In general 泛指某類事物	In particular 描述特定事物
I love **chocolate**. 我喜歡巧克力。	**The chocolate** in this shop is cheap. 這間商店的巧克力很便宜。
Sugar is sweet. 糖是甜的。	Can you pass **the sugar**, please? 可以請你把糖遞過來嗎?
He is still in **hospital** now. 他還在醫院。	We went to **the hospital** to see him. 我們去醫院探望他。

 **Let's try**

Circle the correct words.

請把正確的答案圈出來。

1. (Vegetables / The vegetables) are good for you.

2. Are you interested in (science / the science)?

3. They go to (church / the church) every Sunday.

4. Excuse me, where is (church / the church), please?

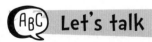 **Let's talk**

What do you think about the following statement? Talk about it.

你對這句話有什麼意見呢?請說一說。

> Not all girls like dolls and not all boys like ball games.

Grammar item 18 | Subject pronouns 主格人稱代名詞

 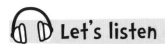 Let's listen

Boy: Who's your best friend?

Girl: Anna is my best friend. I moved here a year ago. I didn't know the kids here. Then I met Anna. She is really kind. We both like to play badminton and since then she and I have always been together.

Boy: Agreed. Anna is so friendly that everyone likes her. She always lets others go before her and she is popular with her friends.

英文能力 UP！

對話中，代名詞（She）用來代替名詞（Anna），避免同樣的名詞不斷重複使用！

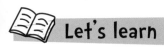 **Let's learn**

We use subject pronouns to replace the name of a person or a thing in the subject position.
主格人稱代名詞用來代替已提及的人或事，放在句子中主語位置。

Singular 單數	I 我	You 你	He 他	She 她	It 它 / 牠
Plural 複數	We 我們	You 你們	They 他們 / 牠們 / 它們		

 **Let's try**

Fill in the blanks with the correct subject pronouns.
請在橫線上填上正確的主格人稱代名詞。

1. My uncle is a driver. _____ has a taxi.

2. My name is Tim. _____ am six years old.

> 這類代名詞通常出現在句子開頭呢！

3. Tracy enjoys reading. _____ has lots of books.

4. There are some monkeys over there. _____ look funny.

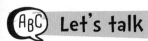 **Let's talk**

Who is your best friend? What is he / she like? What does he / she like? Talk about it.
你最好的朋友是誰？他 / 她是怎樣的？他 / 她喜歡什麼？請説一説。

> My best friend is _____. He / She is
>
> _____. He / She likes _____ .

Grammar item 19 | Object pronouns 賓格人稱代名詞

 Let's listen

Boy: I'm so happy! My mom finally allowed me to have a pet. Look! This is my dear new pet, Chewy.

Girl: He does like eating! Just like you! Taking care of pets is really a difficult job. What do you feed him?

Boy: Fresh vegetables, fruit, and seeds. Well, taking care of him is my responsibility. I love being with him because he's so cute.

英文能力 UP！

動物通常用 it（牠）作代名詞，但人們往往喜歡用 He / him 或 She / her 來代替寵物。

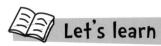

Let's learn

We use object pronouns to replace a noun which is in the object position.

賓格人稱代名詞用來代替已提及的人或事，放在句子賓語位置。

Subject pronouns 主格人稱代名詞	Object pronouns 賓格人稱代名詞	Subject pronouns 主格人稱代名詞	Object pronouns 賓格人稱代名詞
I →	me 我	we →	us 我們
you →	you 你	you →	you 你們
he →	him 他	they →	them 他們
she →	her 她		
it →	it 它 / 牠		

Let's try

Fill in the blanks with the correct object pronouns.

請在橫線上填上正確的賓格人稱代名詞。

> 這類代名詞通常出現在句子末尾呢！

1. Anna is very kind. I like _____.

2. I need to find my book. Where did you put _____?

3. Aunt Lily gave _____ a birthday gift. I really like _____.

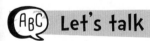

Let's talk

Is there anyone you like in your class? Talk about why you like him / her.

班裏有你喜歡的同學嗎？請説一説你喜歡他 / 她的原因。

_____ is my classmate. I like him / her.

It's because _____.

Grammar item **20** | **Demonstrative pronouns**
指示代名詞

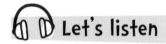 **Let's listen**

Boy: What's that?

Girl: This is a present from my uncle who came over for a visit from America. Let me open it to see what's inside. Wow, how beautiful! I've been wanting to have this more than you know.

Boy: What's so special about this necklace?

Girl: These are precious stones only found in the deep ocean. I'm so, so happy!

英文能力 UP！

對話中的指示代名詞 this 和 these 可以用在句子的開首、中間或結尾，沒有特定的位置。

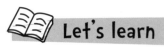

We use *this* and *these* to point to things or people that are close to the speaker. We use *that* and *those* to point to things or people that are more distant from the speaker.

我們用 this、these 指在說話者近處的事物，that、those 指在說話者遠處的事物。

		Examples 例句
Singular 單數	**this** 這個（近處）	**This** is an apple. 這是蘋果。 Come and look at **this**. 來看看這個東西。
	that 那個（稍遠處）	What is **that**? 那是什麼？ **That** is my school bag. 那是我的書包。
Plural 複數	**these** 這些（近處）	Can I have one of **these**? 我可以要其中一個嗎？ **These** are precious stones. 這些是寶石。
	those 那些（稍遠處）	What are **those**? 那些是什麼？ **Those** are my books. 那些是我的書。

 Let's try

Fill in the blanks with the correct demonstrative pronouns.

請在橫線上填上正確的指示代名詞。

1. _____ is my new jacket. Does it look good on me?

2. Thai mangoes are sweeter than _____ from Malaysia.

ABC Let's talk

Everything in your home has a name. Can you name them all? Talk about it.

你能用英語說出家裏所有物件的名字嗎？請說一說。

This / That is _____ (e.g. *a chair*).

These / Those are _____ (e.g. *magazines*).

Grammar item **21** | **Possessive pronouns**
物主代名詞

 Let's listen

Boy: This teddy bear belongs to me. It's mine.

Girl: No, it's not yours. Give it back to Anna. I saw Anna bring it to class. It's hers. There is yours, under the desk.

Boy: Oh no!

Girl: Look at Anna – she's very sad. She's crying. You should say sorry to her.

Boy: I'm so sorry!

英文能力 UP！

有時候，mine、yours、his、hers 等可以放在句子開首，用作強調。
例如 My teddy bear is old. Yours is new and lovely. （我的玩具熊很舊了，你的又新又可愛。）

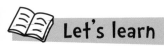 **Let's learn**

We use possessive pronouns to indicate that something belongs to someone.
物主代名詞表示物件是屬於誰的。

Subject pronouns 主格代名詞		Possessive pronouns 物主代名詞
I 我		mine. 我的。
We 我們	have a cup. 有一個杯。	ours. 我們的。
You 你 / 你們		yours. 你的 / 你們的。
They 他們		theirs. 他們的。
She 她	has a cup. 有一個杯。	hers. 她的。
He 他		his. 他的。
It 它 / 牠		its. 它的 / 牠的。

The cup is 這個杯是 →

 Let's try

Fill in the blanks with the correct possessive pronouns.
請在橫線上填上正確的物主代名詞。

1. This car belongs to Mr. and Mrs. Smith. It is _____.

2. This book is _____. It has my name on it.

3. My brother and I made this robot. It is _____.

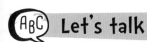 **Let's talk**

Does this belong to your parents? Talk about it.
你身邊有哪些東西是屬於爸爸媽媽的呢？請跟他們説一説。

This _____ belongs to Mommy / Daddy. It's hers / his. Mom / Dad, this _____ is yours.

Grammar item 22 | **Reflexive pronouns** 反身代名詞

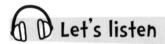 **Let's listen**

Boy: Tonight I'm going to cook for myself.

Girl: Why?

Boy: Mom is not home. Her boss is away and she has to do all the work herself. She needs to work OT.

> overtime 的縮寫，即超時工作

Girl: I see. Are you sure you can take care of yourself? Oh, careful! The pan is very hot. Don't hurt yourself.

英文能力 UP！

I am cooking for myself 是指「我正在給自己做飯」，當中的 myself 不能說成 me，即是不能說 I am cooking for me。此外，I / myself、she / herself 等一般是成對出現的，而 yourself 則是例外，可以省掉做動作的人物，例如 Help yourself.（你自便吧。）

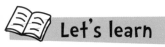

Let's learn

We use reflexive pronouns when the subject and object refer to the same person.

當做動作的和受動作影響的是同一個人，我們就會用反身代名詞。

	Examples 例句
I → **myself** We → **ourselves**	I dried **myself** with a towel. 我用毛巾把自己擦乾。
	We enjoyed **ourselves** very much. 我們玩得很痛快。
You → **yourself**	You should take good care of **yourself**. 你必須好好照顧自己。
He → **himself** She → **herself** It → **itself** They → **themselves**	He hurt **himself**. 他弄傷了自己。
	She talks to **herself**. 她自言自語。
	The birds built **themselves** a nest. 鳥兒為自己築巢。

Let's try

Correct the colored reflexive pronouns.

請改正着色的反身代名詞，然後填在橫線上。

1. She blamed her for the accident. _____

2. I bought me a present. _____

3. This sum is easy. You can do it you. _____

Let's talk

What are the chores that you can do by yourself? Talk about it.

有哪些家務你可以自己獨立完成的呢？請説一説。

I can _____ (e.g. *wipe the floor*) by myself.

Grammar item 23 | Reciprocal pronouns 相互代名詞

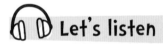 Let's listen

Girl: Do dolphins talk to each other? It seems they do!

Boy: Yes, it sounds like they're whistling to one another.

Girl: I watched the TV program the other day. It said dolphins are able to speak with one another. They don't speak the same way we do, but they still talk. They make special sounds; they also make physical contact and use body language to communicate.

身體接觸

英文能力 UP！

相互代名詞只有兩個，就是對話中的 each other 和 one another，
意思是「互相」、「彼此」。

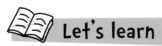 **Let's learn**

A reciprocal pronoun is used when each of two or more persons is acting in the same way toward the other.

當兩個人（或以上）在做同樣的動作，我們就可以用相互代名詞。

Rules 規則	Examples 例子
兩個人 **each other**	Anna and George look at **each other**. 安娜和佐治互相望着對方。
兩個或以上的人 **one another**	The children hug **one another**. 孩子們互相擁抱。
	The dogs sniff **one another**. 那些狗互相嗅對方。

 **Let's try**

Complete the second sentence so that it means the same as the first sentence. Use **each other** or **one another**.

請用 each other 或 one another 來改寫句子，使兩句的意思相同。

1. Anna helped George and George helped Anna.

   Anna and George _____.

2. We sent them a card and they sent us a card.

   We _____.

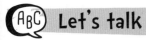 **Let's talk**

Are you doing the best for your family? Talk about it.

在家裏，你是怎樣和其他家庭成員相處呢？請說一說。

In the family, we should _____ one another / each other.

Let's try 答案：1. Anna and George helped each other.　2. We sent a card to one another.

59

Grammar item **24** | **Interrogative pronouns - What / Which**
疑問代名詞

 Let's listen

Boy: Which is the best season for hiking?

Girl: Fall. From barbecues to hiking to camping, there's simply too much to love about this season! What do you think? What is your favorite season?

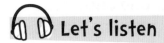
秋天，英式英語叫 autumn

Boy: I like summer because there's no school. And I like warm weather. I go swimming a lot at the beach.

Girl: I like swimming, too. But I hate feeling hot. I'd rather swim in an indoor pool.

英文能力 UP！

What 除了用來發問之外，還可以用來表示感歎，例如 What a lovely day!（多好的天氣啊！）、What nice people they are!（他們人真好啊！）

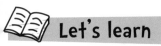

Let's learn

A pronoun that is used to ask a question is called an interrogative pronoun. We use *which* when the number of choices is limited, and use *what* when it is not.

疑問代名詞是用來發問的。當選擇的範圍較小或明確時，會用 which；而當選擇的範圍較大或不明確時，就用 what。

	Examples 例句	Choices 選擇
What 什麼	**What** is 169 divided by 13? 169 除 13 是多少？	/
Which 哪一個	**Which** of the three girls is the oldest? 這三個女孩誰的年齡最大？	3 choices
	Which is bigger – the sun or the earth? 太陽和地球哪個比較大？	2 choices

Let's try

Fill in the blanks with **which** or **what**.

請在橫線上填上 which 或 what。

1. _____ color is your pencil case?

2. _____ is my pen, this one or that one?

3. _____ of these teddy bears do you like best?

Let's talk

How many world capitals do you know? Talk about it with your friend.

你認識多少國家的首都呢？請跟你的朋友互相考考對方吧。

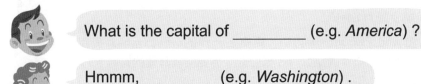

What is the capital of _____ (e.g. *America*) ?

Hmmm, _____ (e.g. *Washington*) .

Let's try 答案：1. What 2. Which 3. Which

Grammar item 25 | Interrogative pronouns - Who / Whose / Whom
疑問代名詞

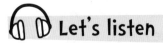 Let's listen

Boy: **Whose** wallet is this?

Girl: Someone might have dropped it. Should we bring it to a nearby business? I think the person will come back through and ask around for it.

Boy: But should we really trust another person to handle the wallet? **Who** can help us? **Whom** should we ask for help?

Girl: Let's call the police to get their advice.

英文能力 UP！

由 who、whom、whose，還有上一課的 what、which 提出的問題
都不能用簡單的 yes / no 來回答，而要回答具體的答案。

 **Let's learn**

We use *who*, *whom*, *whose* to refer to people.

我們用 who, whom, whose 來發問與人有關的問題。

	Ask 問	Answer 答
Who 誰 （做動作的人）	**Who** reads books to you? 誰給你講故事？	**Mom** reads books to me. 媽媽給我講故事。
Whom 誰 （接受動作的人）	**Whom** do you read to? 你給誰講故事？	I read to **baby George**. 我給佐治寶寶講故事。
Whose 誰的	**Whose** book is this? 這是誰的書？	This book is **mine**. 這本書是我的。

 **Let's try**

Fill in the blanks with **who**, **whom** or **whose**.

請在橫線上填上正確的疑問代名詞。

1. _____ should I talk to?

2. _____ umbrella is this?

3. _____ do you think will come first in the race?

在英語口語中，人們一般用 who，而不用 whom。

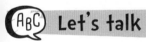 **Let's talk**

Whose is this (are these)? Talk about it with your parents.

這（些）東西是誰的呢？請問一問你的父母吧。

Whose _____ (e.g. *pen*) is this?
Whose _____ (e.g. *books*) are these?

It's / They're _____ (e.g. *Mom's /
Daddy's / mine*) .

Grammar item 26 | The verb *be*
be 動詞

 Let's listen

Boy: What's your name?

Girl: My name is Irina. What's yours?

Boy: My name's Tony. It's nice to meet you, Irina.

Girl: Nice to meet you too. Where're you from?

Boy: I'm from America.

英文能力 UP！

英語口語中會用許多縮略形式，例如 I'm = I am、You're = You are、He's / She's / It's = He is / She is / It is、We're = We are、They're = They are。

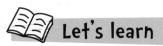 **Let's learn**

The verb *be* has the following forms.

在英語中，be 動詞的意思為「是」，它會根據人或事物（如 I、He、She 等）而有不同的變化。

			be 動詞變化
The first person 第一人稱	單數	I 我	am
	複數	We 我們	are
The second person 第二人稱	單數	You 你	are
	複數	You 你們	are
The third person 第三人稱	單數	He 他	is
		She 她	is
		It 它／牠	is
	複數	They 他們／它們／牠們	are

 **Let's try**

Fill in the blanks with the correct form of **be**.

請在橫線上填上 be 動詞的正確形式。

1. It was warm yesterday, but it _____ very cold today.

2. I _____ at home now. Where _____ you?

Let's talk

Read out and sing this *Verb to Be* song, which uses the same tune as Ten Little Indians.

這是一首 be 動詞的歌曲，請朗讀一遍，然後用《十個小印第安人》的旋律唱出來。

I am, You are, He She It is. I am, You are, He She It is.
I am, You are, He She It is. We are, You are, They are.

Let's try 答案：1. is   2. am; are

Grammar item 27 | Common verbs 一般動詞

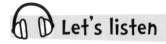 Let's listen

Boy: Let's play charades. Guess what 'action' word I am acting out?

Girl: Hmmm, are you 'eating' something? EAT?

Boy: No. Try again.

Girl: Hmmm, are you 'running' ? RUN?

Boy: You're right. Okay, it's your turn now.

英文能力 UP！

除了 be 動詞以外，其餘動詞都是一般動詞，例如 play、guess、eat、try、run 等吃喝玩樂的動作。

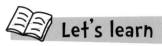 **Let's learn**

A verb is a word that shows action.

動詞是用來表示句中人或物做的動作或行動。

Examples 例子			
eat 吃	drink 喝	read 讀	write 寫
sing 唱歌	dance 跳舞	jump 跳	cry 哭
scream 尖叫	walk 走路	run 跑	sleep 睡覺

 **Let's try**

Circle the verbs in the sentences.

請把句中的動詞圈出來。

> 這些動詞會因不同情況（如時態、人稱等），而出現變化呢！

1. Let's eat sushi today!

2. Anna sings very well.

3. Mr. Smith plays the guitar once a week.

(ABC) Let's talk

Act out some 'action' words and ask your parents to guess the answer. You can use gestures alone.

玩玩猜字遊戲吧！請用動作扮演動詞（參考上表），讓父母猜一猜。

Guess what action word I am acting out?

Let's try 答案：1. eat 2. sings 3. plays

Grammar item **28** | **Verb forms**
動詞形式

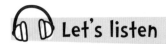

Boy: Let's go swimming in the afternoon, okay?

Girl: I don't want to swim today. I swam yesterday. Today I'll stay at home watching the Olympics. You know, I'm a big fan of Sun Yang.

Boy: Sun Yang! He swims like a fish, doesn't he?

Girl: Yes, he does. He's the greatest swimmer ever! He has swum in the Olympics since he was 17.

英文能力 UP！

中文的動詞沒有形式上的變化，例如昨天、今天、明天「游泳」也好，都是用「游泳」一詞。英語的動詞卻有許多變化，單看 swim 一詞，在不同句子中就有各種不同的形式。

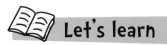

Let's learn

All verbs have five forms.

一般動詞有五種不同的形式。

Base form 原形動詞	Third-person singular 第三人稱單數	Present participle 現在分詞	Past simple 簡單過去式	Past participle 過去分詞
swim	swims	swimming	swam	swum
do	does	doing	did	done
play	plays	playing	played	played
eat	eats	eating	ate	eaten

Let's try

Fill in the blanks with the correct forms of the verb.

請在表格內填上正確的動詞形式。

有些動詞的形式會出現不規則變化，請看一看第 220 - 224 頁的附錄。

e.g. go	goes	going	went	gone
1. walk				
2. drink				

Let's talk

How do you say this in English? Talk about it.

以下句子用英語該怎麼說呢？請說一說。

媽媽喝水。

我喝水。

爸爸正在喝水。

Let's talk 答案：I drink water. / Mom drinks water. / Dad is drinking water.

Let's try 答案：1. walks / walking / walked / walked 2. drinks / drinking / drank / drunk

Grammar item **29** | **Transitive and intransitive verbs**
及物與不及物動詞

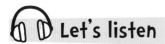 Let's listen

Girl: Of all the creatures on earth, only one can talk like humans. Do you know what it is?

Boy: Yes, I know. Parrots! Parrots can talk.

Girl: That's right. Some parrots can even read. They don't read a book like us, but they learn to read numbers. Scientists say some parrots are even smarter than a two-year-old human.

Boy: Awesome!

英文能力 UP！

在英語中，最簡單的完整句子由「做動作的人 + 動詞」組成，例如 I read. 有些句子的動詞後還會加上其他單詞，即「做動作的人 + 動詞 + 動作涉及的人或物」，例如：I read a book.

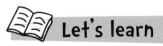

Let's learn

A transitive verb needs a direct object. An intransitive verb does not have an object. Many verbs can be transitive or intransitive.

動詞後面加上動作涉及的人或物是及物動詞，獨立使用的動詞叫不及物動詞。

	Subject 做動作的人	Verb 動詞	Object 動作涉及的人或物	Remark 注意
Transitive verb 及物動詞	Birds	have	wings.	及物動詞後面必須連接動作涉及的人或物，否則句子就不完整。
	I	love	Mom.	
Intransitive verb 不及物動詞	They	laughed.	✕	不及物動詞後面什麼都沒有。
	She	was crying.	✕	

 Let's try

Put **T** (transitive) or **I** (intransitive) in the brackets.

句中的動詞是及物動詞（T），還是不及物動詞（I）呢？請把答案填在括號內。

1. My head aches.   (　　)

2. We enjoyed the play.   (　　)

3. I opened the door.   (　　)

> 有時及物動詞會涉及兩個人或物，例如 He bought me a pencil. 中的 me 和 a pencil 都跟動作有關。

(ABC) Let's talk

How much do you know about the word 'saw'? Read this tongue twister aloud.

你理解這個繞口令的意思嗎？請大聲朗讀出來吧。

see 的過去式（及物動詞）　　　　　　　鋸開（及物動詞）　　鋸（名詞）　　see 的過去式（不及物動詞）

I saw a saw that could out saw any other saw I ever saw.

　　　鋸（名詞）

71

Grammar item 30 | Subject-verb agreement 主動詞一致

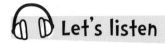

Girl: There are lots of classrooms in our new school. Some of the rooms are special rooms. There is one computer room. There is also a lab. The library is the largest of all.

Boy: There are lots of sports facilities too. I like the basketball court and the covered playground the best.

Girl: I like the garden on the rooftop. We'll have a lot of fun there.

英文能力 UP！

主語跟動詞不一定是連着的，有時需要動動腦筋，想一下哪兩個部分有關係，例如 Some of the rooms are special rooms. 中的 some 顯示是複數，因此這裏用了表示複數的動詞 are。

72

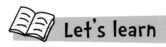 **Let's learn**

The subject and verb must agree in number: both must be singular, or both must be plural.

做動作的人（主語）和動作（動詞）必須一致，必須兩個同時用單數，或同時用複數。

Singular 單數	Plural 複數
There **is** an art **room**. 有一間美術室。	There **are** lots of **classrooms**. 有很多間課室。
Here **comes** the **bus**. 巴士來了。	Here **come** my **classmates**. 我的同學們來了。
He / She does not have a pet. 他 / 她沒有養寵物。	**We / They do** not have a pet. 我們 / 他們沒有養寵物。

 **Let's try**

Circle the correct answers.

請把正確的答案圈出來。

1. One of the children (is / are) sick.

2. Bob (has / have) not done his homework yet.

3. The people in the house (is / are) having a party.

4. Anna and Damian (is / are) going to school together.

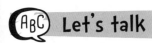 **Let's talk**

How many rooms are there in your home? What are they? Tell a friend about it.

你家裏有多少個房間？那些是什麼房間呢？請跟你的朋友說一說。

There is / are _____ (e.g. *a kitchen / two bedrooms*) in my home.

73

Grammar item 31 | **Three main tenses** 三種主要時態

 Let's listen

Boy: I play table tennis every Sunday. What sports do you play?

Girl: I don't like sports that much, but I played badminton with my cousin yesterday.

Boy: I will play badminton with my friends tomorrow. Will you join us?

Girl: Okay.

英文能力 UP！

對話中，play、played 和 will play 表示了做動作的時間，分別是現在（every Sunday 每個星期天）、過去（yesterday 昨天）和將來（tomorrow 明天）。

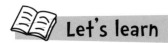 **Let's learn**

Tense means time. There are three main tenses – present tense, past tense and future tense.
時態就是時間的意思，它一般分為現在式、過去式和將來式。

Tenses 時態	Examples 例句
Present 現在	I **play** piano every day. 我每天都彈鋼琴。
Past 過去	I **played** piano yesterday. 我昨天彈鋼琴。
Future 將來	I **will play** piano tomorrow. 我明天會彈鋼琴。

 **Let's try**

Draw lines to connect the sentences.
請把兩組文字串連成句，然後用線連起來。

1. I brush my teeth　　　·　　　·　　A. next week.

2. I talked with Peter　　　·　　　·　　B. every day.

3. I will go to Ocean Park　·　　　·　　C. last night.

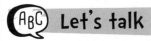 **Let's talk**

Talk about the pictures.
圖中的孩子在做什麼呢？請用提供的詞語說一說。

every day　　　　　last Sunday　　　　next month

75

Grammar item 32 | Present simple - Habitual actions
簡單現在式：慣常動作

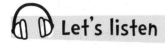 Let's listen

Girl: I eat an apple every day. Mom always told me that 'an apple a day keeps the doctor away'. My sister eats an apple every day, too. Everyone in our family eats an apple a day.

Boy: I've heard that saying ever since I was a little kid, but I don't eat apples.

Girl: Why?

Boy: I once ate a rotten apple and saw a huge worm in it.

英文能力 UP！

就像對話中的女孩每天吃蘋果一樣，我們每天都會刷牙和洗澡，這些情況就要用簡單現在式來表示。

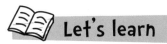 **Let's learn**

We use the present simple to talk about routines – what you do every day or regularly.

簡單現在式用來表示有規律的習慣，即你每天或定期都會做的事情。

Rules 規則	Examples 例句
I, we, you, they + 原形動詞 （什麼都不用轉變）	I **brush** my teeth every morning. 我每天早上刷牙。
	We **live** in America. 我們住在美國。
	They **go** to school by bus. 他們坐巴士上學。
he, she, it + 動詞結尾加 -s 或 -es （動詞以 -s、-x、-ch、 -sh、-o 結尾加 -es）	School **starts** at 8 o'clock in the morning. 課堂在早上八點開始。
	Thomas **goes** to the library every Sunday. 湯瑪士每個星期日都會到圖書館。

 **Let's try**

Circle the correct answers.

請把正確的答案圈出來。

1. They (work / works / workes) until six o'clock.

2. Mom (take / takes / takees) me to school every morning.

3. Tom (watch / watchs / watches) TV every afternoon.

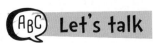 **Let's talk**

What do you do every day or regularly? Talk about it.

你每天或每星期都會做些什麼事情呢？請說一說。

I _____ every day / week, etc.

I _____ every Sunday / Monday, etc.

Let's try 答案：1. work 2. takes 3. watches

Grammar item **33** | **Present simple - Fact or truth**
簡單現在式：事實或真理

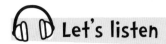

Girl: Wow! Lovely sunrise, isn't it?

Boy: Yes, it's beautiful. Does the sun always rise in the east?

Girl: Yes. For thousands of years, the sun rises in the east, heading to the right, then crosses the high sky, and eventually sets in the west.

Boy: That's so cool. But you have to wake up really early to watch it.

英文能力 UP！

太陽從東方升起、從西方落下，是眾所周知的客觀事實，這些情況會用簡單現在式來表示。

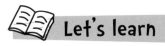 **Let's learn**

We also use the present simple to express a fact or a truth, or things we believe are, or are not, true.

簡單現在式也用來描述客觀的事實或真理，還有那些我們相信或不相信的事情。

Examples 例句
The moon **moves** around the earth. 月亮繞着地球轉。
There **are** twelve months in a year. 一年有十二個月。
Plants **grow** in soil. 植物在泥土中生長。
Water **is** a liquid. 水是液體。

 Let's try

Put **T** (true) or **F** (false) in the brackets.

這些句子說的是事實嗎？是的，請在括號內填 T；不是的，填 F。

1. Horses can talk. ( )

2. Spring follows summer. ( )

3. Watermelons grow on trees. ( )

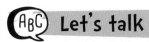 **Let's talk**

What do you know about the earth? Talk about it.

你對地球有多少認識呢？請用以下提示說一說。

☆ What is the shape of the earth?

☆ How many oceans and continents are there on earth?

Grammar item **34** | **Present simple - Negatives**
簡單現在式：否定句

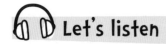

Boy: Chewy doesn't eat anything today. He doesn't run in the wheel for some time, either.

Girl: What happened to him? He doesn't look very happy.

Boy: I don't know. Is he sick?

Girl: He doesn't look sick. I think he's just moody. Hey, Chewy, why don't you talk?

英文能力 UP !

對話中的 don't 和 doesn't 分別是 do not 和 does not 的縮寫，多用於口語中。

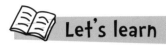

We make negative sentences by adding *do not* or *does not* for the present simple.

簡單現在式用 do not 或 does not 來形成否定句，表達「不」的意思。

I, we, you, they + do not + 原形動詞	
I eat beef. 我吃牛肉。	I **do not** eat beef. 我不吃牛肉。
We lie. 我們說謊。	We **do not** lie. 我們不說謊。
he, she, it + does not + 原形動詞	
Dad smokes. 爸爸抽煙。	Dad **does not** smoke. 爸爸不抽煙。
Anna likes swimming. 安娜喜歡游泳。	Anna **does not** like swimming. 安娜不喜歡游泳。

 **Let's try**

Fill in the blanks with **do not** or **does not**.

請在橫線上填上 do not 或 does not。

1. I _____ stay at home.

2. Our hamster _____ eat apples.

3. We _____ have a family car.

 Let's talk

Ask a friend about his / her likes and dislikes on food. Talk about it.

請訪問一位朋友對不同食物的喜好，然後說一說。

_____ is my friend. He / She likes to eat _____ .

He / She doesn't like to eat _____ .

Grammar item **35** | **Present simple - Questions**
簡單現在式：疑問句

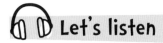 Let's listen

Girl: Do you do sports regularly?

Boy: No, I'm not that much into sports. I'm wondering if I should become more active to exercise and stretch out my muscles. The problem is I hate sports and anything to do with them. I just like to eat.

Girl: Mom says sports are good for our body.

Boy: Does she also say that good food can keep our body looking its best?

英文能力 UP！

I、we、you、they 跟 Do 是一組，he、she、it 則跟 Does 是一組。

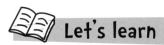 **Let's learn**

We make questions by adding *do* or *does* for the present simple.

簡單現在式用 do 或 does 來提問，組成疑問句。

Do / Does + 人物 + 原形動詞 + ... ?

You watch TV every day. 你每天都看電視。	**Do you** watch TV every day? 你每天都看電視嗎？
They play basketball well. 他們很會打籃球。	**Do they** play basketball well? 他們很會打籃球嗎？
He drinks coffee. 他喝咖啡。	**Does he** drink coffee? 他喝咖啡嗎？

 **Let's try**

Fill in the blanks with **Do** or **Does**.

請在橫線上填上 Do 或 Does。

記住疑問句的末尾要用問號啊！

1. _____ your mother like pizza?

2. _____ you go to school on foot?

3. _____ Peter know how to swim?

4. _____ Mary and Ann go to the library every weekend?

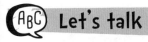 **Let's talk**

What habits do your parents have? Ask them.

你父母有些什麼習慣？請訪問一下他們吧。

 Do you like _____ (e.g. *swimming*)?

 Yes, I do. / No, I don't.

Let's try 答案：1. Does 2. Do 3. Does 4. Do

Grammar item **36** | **Present continuous**
現在進行式

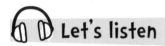 Let's listen

Boy: Hey, come on over! A turtle is laying its eggs.

Girl: It's laying so many eggs. How long does it take an egg to
孵化 (hatch)?

Boy: Probably a few weeks. Look over there! The little
penguins are coming ashore. They are returning from
the sea. They are marching one by one, like an army of
soldiers. Hurrah! Hurrah!

Girl: Hush, don't make so much noise.

英文能力 UP！

現在進行式有時會和動詞 Look!（你看！）、Listen!（你聽！）等同時
出現，提示正在進行的動作。

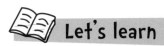 **Let's learn**

The present continuous tense is used to describe an action that is going on.

如果要説這一刻正在做的事情，我們可以用現在進行式。

Rules 規則	Examples 例句
I + am + 動詞 -ing	I **am watching** TV. 我正在看電視。
He / She / It + is + 動詞 -ing	It **is raining**. 現正下雨。
	Anna **is sleeping**. 安娜正在睡覺。
You / We / They + are + 動詞 -ing	We **are singing**. 我們正在唱歌。
	The children **are playing** basketball. 那些孩子正在打籃球。

 **Let's try**

Fill in the blanks with the present continuous tense.

請利用現在進行式，在橫線上填上正確的答案。

> 只要在 am、is、are 後面加上 not，便可把句子變成否定句。

1. I _____ (eat) my breakfast now.

2. The children _____ (swim) in the pool.

3. Look! The elephant _____ (dance) in the rain.

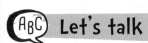 **Let's talk**

What are your parents or friends doing now? Ask them.

請用以下句式來問一問父母或朋友，聽聽他們在做些什麼。

What are you doing now?

I am _____.

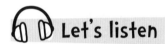 Let's listen

Boy: Look! It's raining again. 不會吧！

Girl: Oh no, not again! It rained all day yesterday too.

Boy: I hate rainy days. I had to stay at home the whole day. It's so boring.

Girl: I stayed at home, too, but I did something fun. I played hide-and-seek with my cousin and then we helped Mom bake cookies.

英文能力 UP！

當我們看見 yesterday（昨天）、last night（昨晚）、last week（上星期）、last month（上個月）、an hour ago（一小時前）等這些表示過去時間的詞語時，那就表示句子裏的動作是在以前發生的。

86

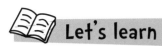

Let's learn

The past simple is used for an action that has already taken place. For regular verbs, we add either *-d* or *-ed* to the verb to create the past tense form.

簡單過去式表示動作是在過去的某個時間裏發生，一般會在動詞後面加 -d 或 -ed 來變成過去式。

Rules 規則	Examples 例句
原形動詞 + -ed	I **cleaned** my room yesterday. 我昨天打掃房間。
以 -e 結尾的動詞 + -d	She **smiled** at me. 她向我微笑。
以 -y 結尾的動詞，先把 y 改成 i，再加上 -ed	The baby **cried** last night. 寶寶昨晚在哭。
短元音或單子音結尾的動詞重複最後的字母，再加上 -ed	She **rubbed** her eyes. 她擦眼睛。

Let's try

Fill in the blanks with the past tense.

請利用過去式，在橫線上填上正確的答案。

> 只要留意動詞的時態變化，就能知道動作發生的大概時間。

1. Mom _____ (bake) a cake yesterday.

2. We _____ (study) very hard for the exam.

3. The car _____ (stop) at the red traffic light.

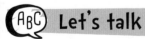

Let's talk

How much do you remember from class yesterday? Talk about it.

你還記得昨天在學校裏做過些什麼事情嗎？請説一説。

> I _____ (e.g. *sang a song*) yesterday.

Grammar item 38 | Past simple - Irregular verbs
簡單過去式：不規則動詞

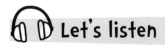 Let's listen

Boy: Something terrible happened to me yesterday.

Girl: What happened?

Boy: I was late for school. I got up too late to catch the school bus. When I ate my breakfast, I spilled the milk all over the table. Nothing went right.

Girl: Oh, poor you!

英文能力 UP！

有些動詞的過去式有各種各樣的變化，例如 get 的過去式不是 getted，而是 got；eat 的過去式不是 eated，而是 ate；spill 的過去式是 spilled，英式說法卻是 spilt；go 的過去式不是 goed，而是 went。

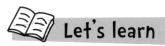

Let's learn

Irregular verbs don't end in *-d* or *-ed* in their past tense. In fact, they don't end in anything in particular.

有些動詞的過去式不是直接加上 -d 或 -ed，這屬於不規則動詞，沒有固定的變化規律。

原形動詞	過去式 （不規則變化）	原形動詞	過去式 （不作任何變化）
buy	bought	cut	cut
have	had	put	put
fall	fell	hurt	hurt
speak	spoke	read	read*

＊注意：讀音出現變化，讀成像「red」。

Let's try

Circle the correct answers.

請把正確的答案圈出來。

> 只要多閱讀，便能記住不規則動詞的過去式。你也看一看第220-224頁的附錄吧。

1. The baby (drank / drink / drinked) all of the milk.

2. We (swims / swimmed / swam) in the pool last week.

3. He (write / wrote / writed) to his grandmother yesterday.

(ABC) Let's talk

Anna is talking about what she did on her birthday. Finish what she says.

安娜在生日那天做了些什麼事情呢？請利用下表説一説。

Morning	do a puzzle
Afternoon	fly a kite
Evening	go to the cinema

Grammar item **39** | **Past simple - Negatives**
簡單過去式：否定句

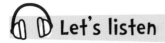 Let's listen

Boy: I didn't see you at Anna's party yesterday.

Girl: I didn't go because I didn't feel very well. I had diarrhea all day and threw up everything I ate. I was so weak that I didn't have any strength. I didn't eat anything, either. I had no at all.　　胃口

Boy: Sorry to hear that. Do you feel any better now?

Girl: Yes, I do.

英文能力 UP！

did not / didn't 已經用了過去式，所以後面的動詞不必改變形式，例如 She didn't go to the party.（她昨天沒有參加派對。）不能說成 She didn't went to the party.

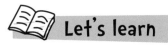

Let's learn

In the past simple, we use *did not / didn't* or *was not / wasn't* and *were not / weren't* for negatives.

在簡單過去式中，我們會用 did not / didn't 、was not / wasn't、were not / weren't 來表示否定。

	Rules 規則	Examples 例句	
Common verbs 一般動詞	**did not / didn't +** **原形動詞** （什麼都不用轉變）	Positives 肯定句	She **ate** an apple. 她吃了一個蘋果。
		Negatives 否定句	She **did not eat** an apple. 她沒有吃蘋果。
Verb *be* be 動詞	•**was not / wasn't** •**were not / weren't**	Positives 肯定句	I **was** happy. 我很開心。
		Negatives 否定句	I **was not** happy. 我不開心。

Let's try

Rewrite the sentences using the negatives.

請把句子改寫成否定句，填在橫線上。

1. We invited her to the party.

_____

2. The children were interested in the movie.

_____

Let's talk

What was it like to be a child in the past? Ask your partents or grandparents, then talk about it.

你知道以前的孩子是怎樣生活的嗎？請用以下提示訪問你父母或祖父母，然後説一説。

☆ computer   ☆ television   ☆ smartphones

Let's try 答案：1. We did not / didn't invite her to the party.
2. The children were not / weren't interested in the movie.

91

Grammar item **40** | **Past simple - Questions**
簡單過去式：疑問句

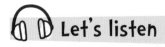

Boy: What did you do last Sunday?

Girl: I went to the Peak on a field trip. I didn't enjoy it because I've been there a lot with my mom. But I enjoyed playing and picnicking with my classmates.

Boy: Did you go to the Wax Museum? They've got some new figures on display.

Girl: No, I didn't. I missed it.

英文能力 UP !

用 Did...? 來發問的疑問句，可用簡單的 yes/no 來回答，或回應 Yes, I did. / No, I didn't.

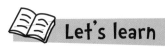 **Let's learn**

In the past simple questions, we use *Did...?* or *What / Where / Why did...?*

在簡單過去式中，我們用 Did...? 或 What / Where / Why did...? 等來發問。

Ask 問	Answer 答
What did you do at Christmas? 你在聖誕節做了些什麼事情？	I **went** to... 我去了……
Where did you have the party? 你在哪裏開派對？	I **had** the party at... 我在……開派對。
Why did she come early? 為什麼她早了來到？	She **came** early because... 她早了來到是因為……
Did you have a big dinner? 你有吃一頓聖誕大餐嗎？	No, I **didn't**. （我）沒有。

 Let's try

Unscramble the sentences.

請重組句子，填在橫線上。

> 當句子中的是 be 動詞時，就可組成 Was / Were...? 或 What was / were...? 等的疑問句。

1. Did you / Anna / in / see / the / library / ?

_____

2. TV / on / watch / What / did / you / night / last / ?

_____

(ABC) Let's talk

Imagine that a friend has just come back from holiday. Ask him / her about it.

假設你的朋友剛剛從外地旅遊回來，請用以下句式訪問他/她。

 Where did you go?
Did you meet any interesting people?

Let's try 答案：1. Did you see Anna in the library? 2. What did you watch on TV last night?

Grammar item 41 | Past continuous 過去進行式

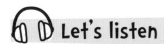 Let's listen

Boy: How come you didn't answer when I called you?

Girl: Huh? When?

Boy: Last night. Were you home? I was ringing and ringing for you the whole evening and you were not answering at all.

Girl: Oh I'm sorry. I was with Mom and Dad. We were watching TV all evening. I guess I didn't hear the phone.

英文能力 UP！

既然「現在進行式」是指「現在這一刻正在做的事情」，那麼只需要把「現在」換成「過去」，就是「過去進行式」啦！

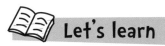

Let's learn

The past continuous tense is used for an action that was going on in the past.

當我們要説明過去某時刻正在做的事情時，就會用過去進行式。

Rules 規則	Examples 例句
I + was + 動詞 -ing	I was sleeping. 那時我正在睡覺。
He / She / It + was + 動詞 -ing	The dog was barking. 那時狗在吠叫。 Dad was working. 那時爸爸在工作。
You / They / We + were + 動詞 -ing	They were reading in the library. 那時他們正在圖書館閱讀。 We were having dinner. 那時我們正在吃晚餐。

Let's try

Fill in the blanks with the past continuous tense.

請利用過去進行式，在橫線上填上正確的答案。

1. Thomas _____ (ride) a bicycle.

2. I _____ (watch) TV in the living room.

3. The children _____ (play) hide-and-seek in the playground.

Let's talk

Look at some old photos of yours. Do you remember what you were doing in the photos? Talk about it.

找一些舊照片來看看，還記得照片中的你在做什麼嗎？請説一説。

I was _____ in this photo.

| Grammar item | 42 | Simple future - will
簡單將來式 |

Let's listen

Boy: I think I will be a vet when I grow up.

Girl: A vet? Really? Why? ~veterinarian 的縮寫，即獸醫

Boy: I love animals. I'll help them. I'll have lots of pets –
       grasshoppers, beetles, spiders, lizards and even snakes.
       What about you?

Girl: Oh no, I don't think I'll be a vet. I have a fear of lizards
       and snakes. I can't stand those scaly creatures lurking
       around me. I shall be a teacher. I'll teach children.

英文能力 UP！

在英語中，will 的意思是「將會」，它的縮寫是 'll，例如 I'll、She'll、
We'll、They'll 等。在口語中，我們較常用它的縮寫。

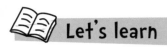 **Let's learn**

The future tense is used for an action that has yet to take place or will take place in the future. We use *will* or *shall* to talk about the future in general.

那些仍未發生，但預期會在將來發生的事情，需要使用將來式來表示。使用時，我們一般會加上 will 或 shall 。

Rules 規則	Examples 例句
I / We + shall **+ 原形動詞**	I **shall finish** my homework soon. 我馬上就會把作業完成。
I / We / You / He / **She / It / They +** **will + 原形動詞**	Tomorrow **will be** a holiday. 明天是假期。 He **will watch** a movie an hour later. 他一個小時後會去看電影。 They **will go** to the museum next Sunday. 他們下星期日會去博物館。

注意：當 will 前面的詞語是 I 或 we（第一人稱）時，便可用 shall 來代替。

 **Let's try**

Circle the correct answers.

請把正確的答案圈出來。

1. Mr. Smith (will flew / shall fly / will fly) to Beijing next week.

2. We (shall meet / will met / will be meet) at the cinema tonight.

3. They (shall play / will play / will be played) basketball on Sunday.

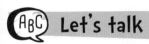 **Let's talk**

What do you want to be when you grow up? Talk about it.

你將來想做什麼呢？請利用以下句式説一説。

I will / shall be a / an _____ when I grow up.

I will / shall _____.

Grammar item **43** | **Simple future - Negatives**
簡單將來式：否定句

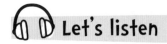 **Let's listen**

Girl: I'm so excited. The talent show next week is going to be fun. Who do you think will win?

Boy: I don't know. I won't join the talent show.

Girl: Why? I thought you'll put on a taekwondo performance with Bob.

Boy: No. Bob has sprained his ankle badly and I'm afraid he won't be able to go on stage next week.

英文能力 UP！

will not 的否定形式不是 willn't，而是 won't，注意不要寫錯啊！

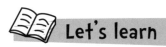

Let's learn

The negative of will is *will not*, or *won't*, which is used to express something you are not willing to do, or something will not happen.

will 的否定形式是 will not，或縮寫作 won't。我們用它來表達不想做，或不會發生的事情。

	人物 + **will not** + 原形動詞
I **will be** late. 我會遲到。	I **will not / won't be** late. 我不會遲到。
The dog **will bite** you. 這隻狗會咬你的。	The dog **will not / won't bite** you. 這隻狗不會咬你的。
We **will visit** Japan in June. 我們六月會去日本旅遊。	We **will not / won't visit** Japan in June. 我們六月不會去日本旅遊。

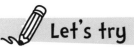

Let's try

Rewrite the sentences using the negatives.
請把句子改寫成否定句，填在橫線上。

1. I will lend you my bicycle.

_____

2. Aunt will come to visit us this summer.

_____

Let's talk

Is there anything you won't do to your friends? Talk about it.
你不會對朋友做哪些事情呢？請説一説。

I won't _____ (e.g. *lie to*) my friends.

Let's try 答案：1. I will not / won't lend you my bicycle.
2. Aunt will not / won't come to visit us this summer.

99

Grammar item **44** | **Simple future - Questions**
簡單將來式：疑問句

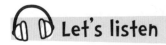

Boy: What will the earth look like in the future?

Girl: Teacher says the earth is sick now. The climate is changing and there's no future if we keep polluting the environment.

Boy: Oh, will the climate keep changing or will it go back to normal? What will happen if we keep polluting the environment? What shall we do in order to help save the earth?

Girl: Teacher says we should protect our earth.

英文能力 UP！

shall 的疑問句是用來提出意見，或請對方做決定，例如 Shall I open the window?（要我開窗嗎？）、What shall we do?（我們該怎麼做？），詳見第 146 - 147 的內容。

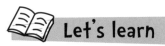 **Let's learn**

We make questions by using *Will...?* or *What / Where / Why will...?* for the future tense.

簡單將來式一般用 Will...? 或 What / Where / Why will...? 等來提問將來發生的事情。

	Ask 問	Answer 答
Will...?	**Will you** help me with this? 你可以幫忙拿這個嗎？	Yes, I **will**. （我）可以。
	Will you go to Anna's birthday party? 你會參加安娜的生日會嗎？	No, I **won't**. （我）不會。
What will...?	**What will** you / Anna do next Saturday? 你 / 安娜下星期六會做些什麼？	I / She **will**... 我 / 她將會……

 **Let's try**

Unscramble the sentences.

請重組句子，填在橫線上。

1. go / Where / for the holidays / will you / ?

_____

2. Will / the hairdresser / you / tomorrow / go to / ?

_____

 Let's talk

Read a story book with your parents and guess what will happen next. Talk about it.

請跟父母一起閱讀故事書，邊讀邊猜測故事發展，然後說一說。

What do you think will happen on the next page?

Hmmm, _____.

Let's try 答案：1. Where will you go for the holidays?
2. Will you go to the hairdresser tomorrow?

> Grammar item **45** | **Future - be going to**
> 用 be going to 表示將來

🎧 Let's listen

Girl: Hey, what are you doing?

Boy: I am going to plant a tree. Can you help me?

Girl: Sure. Let's dig a hole in the ground first, okay?

Boy: I already did that. Ooh ooh look out! You're going to fall!

Girl: Ouuch!

英文能力 UP !

與 will 一樣，句式 am / is / are going to 也是用來表達未來會發生的事情。在大多數情況下，兩個用法是互通的。但相對於 will 而言，am / is / are going to 提及的事情發生的機會較高。

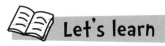 **Let's learn**

We use *am / is / are going to* to talk about something we plan to do in the very near future or something that will clearly happen soon.

我們用 am / is / are going to 來說明計劃去做的事情，或必然會發生的事情。

做動作的人 / 物 + **be**	+ **going to**	+ 原形動詞
I **am**		**swim** in the afternoon. 我將會在下午游泳。
It **is**	going to	**rain** soon. 快要下雨了。
He / She **is**		**play** basketball. 他 / 她將會打籃球。
We / You / They **are**		**bake** some cookies. 我們 / 你們 / 他們準備烤曲奇餅。

 Let's try

Connect the sentences.

請配對以下句子，然後用線連起來。

注意這些縮寫：
I am = I'm
He / She is = He / She's
We / They are = We / They're

1. Look at the sky. •

2. John does not have an umbrella. •

• A. He's going to get wet.

• B. It's going to rain.

(ABC) Let's talk

George is talking about what he's going to do in the coming five days. Finish what he says.

佐治在未來五天將要做些什麼事情呢？請根據以下提示說一說。

Monday	Tuesday	Wednesday	Thursday	Friday
book	**piano**	**swimming**	**basketball**	**movie**

Grammar item **46** | **Questions - be going to**
用 be going to 形成疑問句

 Let's listen

Boy: What are you going to do?

Girl: I'm going to the library. What about you?

Boy: I'm gonna do one hour of volunteer work. I signed up

going to 的
口語用法

to be a volunteer and today I'm going to pick up litter around the school. Are you going to join me?

Girl: No, I've got to go to the library right away.

英文能力 UP！

留意句式「I'm going to＋原形動詞」是將來式的用法，而對話中的 I'm going to the library.（我正在去圖書館。）是現在進行式。

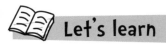 **Let's learn**

When asking questions about the future with *be going to*, you can ask questions like:

當我們提問關於將來的事情，可以使用以下句式：

Ask 問	Answer 答
Are you going to play football with us? 你會跟我們一起踢足球嗎？	**Yes**, I am. / **No**, I am not. （我）會。/ 不會。
Is Dad going to play football with us? 爸爸會跟我們一起踢足球嗎？	**Yes**, he is. / **No**, he isn't. （他）會。/ 不會。
What are you going to do after school? 下課以後你會做些什麼呢？	**I'm going to** go home. 我會回家。
Where are you going to have dinner? 你會去哪裏吃晚餐？	**I'm going to** eat at home. 我會在家裏吃晚餐。

 **Let's try**

Write questions with **going to**.

請根據提示，利用 going to 來寫疑問句，填在橫線上。

1. The sky is full of black clouds. (rain?)

   _____

2. I have bought a painting. (Where / hang it?)

   _____

 Let's talk

What are your parents going to do this weekend? Ask them.

你父母周末有些什麼計劃呢？請用以下句式問一問他們。

> Are you going to _____ this weekend?

Grammar item 47 | **Present perfect** 現在完成式

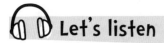

Girl: What are you doing?

Boy: I'm looking for my lunchbox. I can't find it anyway. I have lost my lunchbox. Someone has stolen it.

Girl: There it is, on the floor. Oh, it's empty. Someone has eaten your food!

Boy: My goodness! Look at these footprints on the floor. What a naughty dog!

英文能力 UP！

對話中的 has、have 不是「有」的意思，而是在現在完成式中表示「已經」完成了某件事情。

106

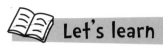 **Let's learn**

We form the present perfect with *has / have + the past participle*, which is always a link between the past and the present.

我們會用 has / have + 過去分詞，來說明從過去直到現在這刻的事情。

Usage 用法	做動作的人／物 + **has / have** + 過去分詞
Completed action 完成的動作	I **have eaten** my lunch. 我已經吃完午飯。
	He **has finished** his homework. 他已經做完了功課。
Experience 經驗	I **have seen** the movie. 我曾經看過那部電影。
	Jane **has been** to America. 珍曾經到過美國。
Continuous situation 持續的情況	I **have lived** in America for ten years. 我在美國住了十年。
	He **has been** ill since last week. 他從上周起一直生病。

 **Let's try**

Fill in the blanks with the present perfect tense.

請利用現在完成式，在橫線上填上正確的答案。

> 請看一看第 220 - 224 頁的附錄，認識不同動詞的過去分詞。

1. I _____ (lose) my key.

2. Aunt Carol _____ (go) to Australia.

Let's talk

Have you ever been to these places? Tell a friend about it.

你去過這些地方嗎？請用以下句式，跟朋友說一說。

> Have you ever been to _____ (e.g. *the Peak*)?

> Yes, I have been there (e.g. *once / twice*).
> No, I have never been there.

Grammar item **48** | **Present perfect continuous**
現在完成進行式

 Let's listen

Boy: It's been so hot these days. What have you been doing with your free time recently?

Girl: I've been doing a lot of reading these days.

Boy: What are some of your favorite books that you've been reading lately?

Girl: I've been reading the Grimm's Fairy Tales. They are very interesting.

格林童話

英文能力 UP！

It's been... 用來指事情已經發生了一段頗長時間，例如 It's been so hot these days. （最近都是那麼熱啊。）在日常生活中，跟許久沒見的人打招呼時，也可以說一句：Hey, it's been a while. （嘿，好久不見了。）

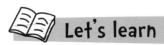 **Let's learn**

We use the present perfect continuous when we talk about an action which began in the past and is still happening.

當我們從過去開始做某個動作，一直持續到現在這一刻，看來還會繼續做下去，便要用現在完成進行式。

做動作的人/物 + **has / have been** + 動詞 -ing	
與 **since** 連用： 表示從某個時間開始	I have been watching TV since three o'clock. 我從三點開始一直在看電視。
與 **for** 連用： 表示持續一段時間	It has been raining for two days. 雨下了兩天。
How long + **has / have** + 做動作的人/物 + **been** + 動詞 -ing？	
與 **how long** 連用： 用來發問	How long have you been learning English? 你學英語學了多久？

 **Let's try**

Circle the correct answers.

請把正確的答案圈出來。

> 現在完成進行式
> 表示的持續情況
> 一般是短暫的。

1. The baby (has been crying / has crying) for an hour.

2. Justin has been playing the piano (since / for) he was three.

3. How long (you have been / have you been) waiting?

 Let's talk

Have you been learning to play a musical instrument or sport? Talk about it.

你有學習樂器或體育運動嗎？請說一說。

> I've been _____ since I was _____ (e.g. *three*).
> I've been _____ for _____ (e.g. *two years*).

Grammar item 49 | Positions of adjectives 形容詞的位置

 Let's listen

Girl: Look carefully at this work of art. What do you see? Does it remind you of anything in real life?

Boy: Hmm, I see something like a seal. A blue seal. What about you?

Girl: I see an old man. He looks angry. I think he feels lonely. Maybe he is living an unhappy life.

Boy: You see a lot! You're so full of imagination!

英文能力 UP！

當我們用許多不同的英文單詞來描述一個事物的外觀，或給我們的感覺，那時說出來的就是 adjective 形容詞了！

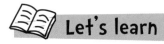 **Let's learn**

We use adjectives before nouns and after a few verbs
(especially **be**).

形容詞常常會放在不同的位置，它有時會在名詞前面，有時會在 be 動
詞或與我們的感官有關的動詞後面。

Positions 位置	Examples 例子		
Before nouns 名詞前面	an **old** shirt 舊襯衫	a **yummy** soup 美味的湯	a **narrow** street 狹窄的街道
After the verb *be* be 動詞後面	I am **happy**. 我開心。	He is **angry**. 他生氣。	They are **hungry**. 他們餓了。
After verbs of perception 感官動詞後面	feel **tired** 感到疲累 look **funny** 看來很有趣	smell **good** 氣味很香 seem **nice** 覺得不錯	taste **sweet** 味道很甜 sound **strange** 聽起來很怪

 **Let's try**

Unscamble the sentences.

請重組句子，填在橫線上。

1. was / roller coaster / The / exciting

_____.

2. Bob / a / backpack / bought / blue

_____.

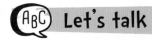 **Let's talk**

Use three adjectives to describe a person you know well.
Talk about him / her.

請用三個形容詞來形容一個你認識的人，然後説一説。

My mom / dad / etc. is _____, _____ and _____.

Grammar item 50 | **Kinds of adjectives** 形容詞的種類

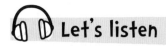

Boy: Look! There's a square pond with a glass fountain over there!

Girl: And there's a grey dragon with a very long tail flying in the sky!

Boy: Is it a Chinese dragon or a Western dragon?

Girl: I don't know, but everything looks so weird in here!

英文能力 UP！

描述事物時，我們可以從它的尺寸（size）、給人的感覺或特徵（quality or opinion）、顏色（color）、形狀（shape）、產地（origin）、物料（material）等入手，準確地把事物描繪出來。

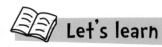

Let's learn

A descriptive adjective is used to provide more information to a noun (a person, a thing, an animal or a place) by describing it.

當我們對人物、事物、動物、地方等的名稱一無所知時，形容詞能提供更多資訊。

Usage 用法	Examples 例子	
Size 尺寸	a **high** mountain 高山	**long** hair 長髮
Quality or opinion 給人的感覺或特徵	a **beautiful** girl 漂亮的女孩	a **sunny** day 晴天
Color 顏色	a **red** car 紅色的車	a **black** cat 黑貓
Shape 形狀	**round** eyes 圓圓的眼睛	an **oval** seed 橢圓形的種子
Origin 國籍或產地	a **Japanese** TV 日本製電視	a **Chinese** temple 中式廟宇
Material 物料	a **wooden** table 木桌子	a **plastic** bag 塑料袋

Let's try

Use three adjectives to describe this dragon.

請用三個形容詞來描述這條龍，填在橫線上。

✦ —————

✦ —————

✦ —————

Let's talk

How would you describe the weather where you are today? Talk about it.

你會怎樣形容今天的天氣呢？請說一說。

It's _____ (e.g. *sunny / rainy / cloudy / foggy*) today.

Grammar item 51 | Order of adjectives 形容詞的詞序

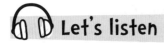

Boy: Have you found anything nice yet?

Girl: I love this doll. She's really cute. I want to have beautiful long blonde hair like her. What about you?

Boy: I got this giant Japanese alloy robot. Does it look cute?

Girl: It looks so adorable.

英文能力 UP！

描述事物時，使用二至四個形容詞已經很足夠。再多的話，句子便會變得難於閱讀。

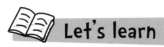 **Let's learn**

Sometimes we use two or more adjectives together.
Opinion adjectives usually go before fact adjectives.

為了給事物提供豐富的資訊，有時候我們會把兩個或更多形容詞連在
一起使用。表示意見的形容詞一般放在前面，描述事物的則放在後面。

	Adjectives 形容詞						Nouns 名詞
Opinion 意見	**Fact 事實**						
	Size 尺寸	**Age 年歲**	**Shape 形狀**	**Color 顏色**	**Origin 產地或國籍**	**Material 物料**	
a delicious							soup
a beautiful	large		square			wooden	table
a	small			black		plastic	bag
an		old			Japanese		song
	big		round	blue			eyes

 **Let's try**

Put the adjectives in brackets in the correct position.

請把括號內的形容詞放在適當的位置，然後填在橫線上。

1. a red jacket (leather) _____

2. a little village (lovely / old) _____

3. a big cat (fat / black) _____

 **Let's talk**

Ask your parents to guess what you're describing.

請用形容詞描述一個物件，讓你父母猜一猜。

 It is _____ . Guess what?

Grammar item **52** | **Adjectives ending in *-ing* and *-ed***
以 -ing 和 -ed 結尾的形容詞

 Let's listen

Boy: You've read this book many times. Are you bored?

Girl: Not at all. The book is full of beautiful imagery that makes
一點也不 you feel as if you were actually there. The characters are
so interesting. It has a good amount of dialogue, but not so
much as to make you feel bored.

Boy: Can I have a look?

Girl: Here you are. Read it. It's not boring. You will be interested.

英文能力 UP！

bored 與 boring，或 interested 與 interesting 的用法很易混淆。它們都
是形容詞，但對話中的 bored 與 interested 指人，例如我覺得很悶或
很感興趣；而 boring 與 interesting 則指事物，即它很沉悶或有趣。

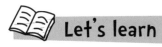

Let's learn

There are many pairs of adjectives ending in *-ing* and *-ed*. Someone is *-ed* if something (or someone) is *-ing*. Or, if something is *-ing*, it makes you *-ed*.

不少形容詞會成雙成對地出現，它們以 -ed 或以 -ing 來結尾，分別用來描述人的情緒和令人感到該情緒的事物或人。

An emotion 人的情緒	frightened 驚慌	annoyed 厭煩	amazed 驚訝
Something / someone caused the emotion 令人感到該情緒的 事物或人	frightening 令人驚慌的	annoying 令人厭煩的	amazing 令人驚訝的

Let's try

Circle the correct adjectives.

請把正確的形容詞圈出來。

1. This TV program is (bored / boring).

2. George is (interested / interesting) in science.

3. Everyone was (surprised / surprising) that he came.

4. I enjoyed the roller coaster ride. It was quite (excited / exciting).

Let's talk

Have you read a book recently? Did you find it interesting? Talk about it.

你最近有看書嗎？那些書有趣嗎？請用以下句式説一説。

Yes, the book was interesting. It is because _____.

No, the book was boring. It is because _____.

Grammar
item **53** | **Adjectives of comparison**
形容詞比較級

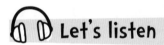 **Let's listen**

Boy: I have one elder sister and one younger brother. My sister is one year older than me and my brother is four years younger than me.

Girl: I'm an only child. I really envy you who have both a brother and a sister.

Boy: But sometimes it's annoying to take care of my baby brother. He cries all the time.

Girl: You should try to get along with him.

英文能力 UP！

My brother is younger than me（弟弟年紀比我小。）不能説成 My brother is more young than me。

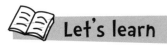 **Let's learn**

Comparative adjectives compare two things.

當我們比較兩個性質相同的事物時，就會用到形容詞的比較級。

Rules 規則	Examples 例句
一般單音節形容詞： 在詞尾加 -er	A is tall**er than** B. A 比 B 高。
以 -e 結尾的單音節形容詞： 在詞尾加上 -r	A is large**r than** B. A 比 B 大。
短元音或單子音結尾的單音節 形容詞： 重複最後的字母，再加上 -er　　+ than	A is big**ger than** B. A 比 B 大。
以 -y 結尾的雙音節形容詞： 先把 y 改成 i，再加上 -er	A is heav**ier than** B. A 比 B 重。
其他雙音節或多音節詞： 在形容詞前加上 more	A is **more** interesting **than** B. A 比 B 有趣。

 **Let's try**

Fill in the blanks with comparative adjectives.

請利用形容詞的比較級，在橫線上填上正確的答案。

1. You look a little _____ (fat)
   than before. Have you gained weight?

   > 比較級前面還可以加上 a
   > lot、much、a little 等來突
   > 顯兩個事物的分別。

2. Let's buy this one. It's a lot _____ (cheap).

 Let's talk

Compare the sizes of any two different vehicles. Talk
about it.

請用以下句式比較兩種交通工具的大小，然後説一説。

> A / An _____ (e.g. *airplane*) is (a lot) bigger
> than a /an _____ (e.g. *car*) .

Let's try 答案：1. fatter　2. cheaper

119

Grammar item 54 | Superlative adjectives 形容詞最高級

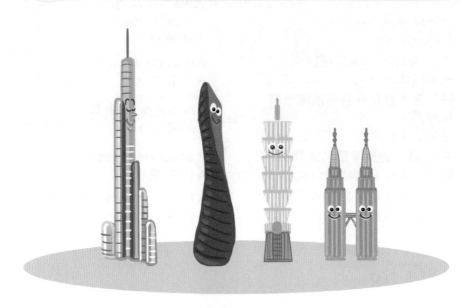

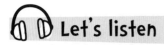 Let's listen

Boy: Do you know where the tallest building in the world is?

Girl: I heard it is in a desert, is it?

Boy: You're right. It's in Dubai. It's called Burj Khalifa. It has 169 stories. It also has the highest observation deck off the ground.
樓層

Girl: And I heard people are doing bungee jumping from the tallest buildings in the world. Sounds scary, doesn't it?

英文能力 UP！

This is the tallest building. （這是最高的建築物。）不能説成 This is the most tall building.

 **Let's learn**

Superlative adjectives compare more than two things. We use them to say which thing is top in a group.

比較三個或更多性質相同的事物時，用最高級來表示「最……的一個」。

Rules 規則		Examples 例句
the	一般單音節形容詞： 在詞尾加 -est	This is **the tallest** building. 這座是最高的建築物。
	以 -e 結尾的單音節形容詞： 在詞尾加上 -st	This is **the largest** jacket. 這件是最大的外套。
	短元音或單子音結尾的單音節形容詞： 重複最後的字母，再加上 -est	This is **the biggest** stone. 這塊是最大的石頭。
	以 -y 結尾的雙音節形容詞： 先把 y 改成 i，再加上 -est	This is **the heaviest** bag. 這個是最重的袋子。
	其他雙音節或多音節詞： 在形容詞前加上 most	This is **the most** interesting book. 這本是最有趣的書。

 **Let's try**

Fill in the blanks with superlative adjectives.

請利用形容詞的最高級，在橫線上填上正確的答案。

1. She's _____ (clever) girl in the school.

2. It's _____ (boring) movie I've ever seen.

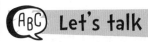 **Let's talk**

Surf the net about the Guinness World Records. Talk about it with your friends.

請在網上尋找健力士世界紀錄的資料，然後跟你的朋友互相考考對方。

Who is the _____ (e.g. *tallest man*) in the world?

121

Grammar item 55 | Irregular comparatives and superlatives 比較級和最高級的不規則變化

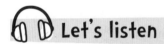 Let's listen

Girl: Of all the students in my class, Colin is the best in Math.

Boy: I know him. He is popular with his friends. He got the Math Award last year.

Girl: He's the smartest guy I've ever known. He can do the most difficult sums really quickly.

Boy: But he is poor at art. His drawings are the worst I have ever seen.

英文能力 UP！

good 的比較級和最高級並不是 gooder 和 goodest；bad 的比較級和最高級也不是 badder 和 baddest。

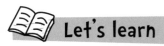

Let's learn

Some adjectives have different forms of comparatives and superlatives. They do not end in *-er* or *-est*, or add *more* or *most* in the front.

有些形容詞的比較級和最高級不是在後面加上 -er 或 -est，也不是在前面加上 more 或 most，而是完全變成另外一個單詞！

Adjectives 形容詞	Comparatives 比較級	Superlatives 最高級
good 好	better 好一些	best 最好
bad 差；壞	worse 差一些；壞一些	worst 最差；最壞

Let's try

Correct the sentences.

請改正句子，然後填在橫線上。

1. I think summer is best than winter.

_____

2. The problem got worser and worser.

_____

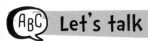

Let's talk

What is your best and worst subject? Talk about it.

你最好和最差的學科分別是什麼呢？請説一説。

My best / worst subject is _____.

Let's try 答案：1. I think summer is better than winter.
2. The problem got worse and worse.

123

Grammar item 56 | Comparison with *(not) as...as*
用（not）as...as 作同級比較

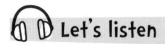 Let's listen

Girl: Who is the tallest in your class?

Boy: Justin and Heinrich are the tallest. They are taller than any other student. But they aren't as tall as Mr. Smith, our class teacher.

Girl: Are they of the same age?

Boy: Yes, Justin is the same age as Heinrich. They are twin brothers.

英文能力 UP！

A is the same age as B. 指「A 和 B 的年齡一樣」，它的另一個正確的說法是 Justin is as old as Heinrich. 有人會把這句話說成 Justin is the same age like Heinrich. ，但這是錯誤的。

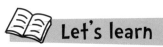

Let's learn

We use *as...as* and *not as...as* to make comparisons. *as... as* can be used in positive sentences and in questions.

我們會用 as...as 和 not as...as 來比較兩個相似或不相似的事物。其中 as...as 能組成肯定句和疑問句。

Usage 用法		Examples 例句
as...as 和……一樣	**Positives** 肯定句	The world's biggest cat is **as tall as** a man. 世界上最大的貓跟人一樣的高。
	Questions 疑問句	Is this comic book **as** funny **as** that book? 這本漫畫書跟那本一樣有趣嗎？
not as...as 不像……那樣	**Negatives** 否定句	This mango is **not as** sweet **as** that one. 這個芒果不及那個甜。

Let's try

Fill in the blanks with **(not) as...as**.

請根據提示，利用 (not) as...as 完成句子，填在橫線上。

1. Mary is _____ (not / hardworking) Carol.

2. Will robots be _____ (clever) humans in the future?

3. This cake is _____ (not / yummy) the one I bought yesterday.

Let's talk

Look these words up in your dictionary and talk about their meanings.

as...as 經常用作比喻，你認識以下兩個短語嗎？請翻查詞典，然後説一説它們的意思吧。

✿ as busy as a bee   ✿ as stubborn as a mule

Grammar item **57** **Adjectives as nouns**
用作名詞的形容詞

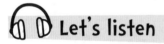

Boy: This is my design of the dream city. This large park is designed for the old and the retired. This hospital is for the sick and the injured.

Girl: What is this?

Boy: This is the Water World. It is a large playground for the young. We can do lots of things here.

Girl: Wow, I hope your dream will come true.

英文能力 UP！

the old 和 the young 代表一類人，因此它們跟複數動詞連用，例如我們會説 The rich help the poor.（有錢人幫助窮人。），而不説 The rich helps the poor.

Let's learn

The structure of *the + adjective* is used to talk about some well-known groups of people.

我們可以在某些形容詞前面加上 the，令它變成名詞，用來表示一些特定類別的人。

Usage 用法	Examples 例子	
Groups of people 某一類人	the old 老人 (= old people)	the young 年輕人 (= young people)
	the blind 盲人 (= blind people)	the deaf 聾人 (= deaf people)
Nationalities 某國籍的人	the Chinese 中國人 (= Chinese people)	the Americans 美國人 (= American people)

Let's try

Put **A** (adjective) or **N** (noun) in the brackets.

句中着色的單詞是形容詞（A）還是名詞（N）？請把答案填在括號內。

1. He is a poor man. ( )

2. He always helps the poor. ( )

3. The nurse is caring for the sick. ( )

4. Mom doesn't feel well. She's sick. ( )

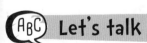

Let's talk

Read this tongue twister aloud.

請大聲朗讀這個繞口令吧。

> This chef is deaf, but he's the best among the deaf.

Grammar item 58 | Use *can* to show ability
用 can 表示能力

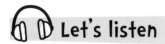

Boy: Let's row a boat across the lake.

Girl: No, I can't row a boat. Hey, I can hear a strange noise. It sounds like a strange gurgling sound coming from underwater. Can you hear it?

Boy: Yes, that's mysterious. What could that be?

Girl: Oh, look! The water is bubbling furiously! It could be a sea monster. Let's run!

英文能力 UP！

對話中的 can 是情態動詞（modal），能給動詞添加額外的意思。

Section 7 將會介紹不同的情態動詞。

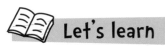 **Let's learn**

We use *can* to talk about someone's skill or general abilities. For the negatives, we can use *cannot* or *can't*.

我們用 can 來說明人們的技能或能力。表示否定的意思時，會用 cannot 或 can't。

Usage 用法	Examples 例句
can 會 / 能夠	I **can speak** English. 我會講英文。 **Can** you **swim**? 你會游泳嗎？
cannot / can't 不能	He **cannot do** the sum. 他不懂計算這條加數。 She **can't spell** the word correctly. 她不能把單詞正確地拼出來。

 **Let's try**

Fill in the blanks with the correct verbs. Use **can** or **can't**.

請選出正確的動詞，並加上 can 或 can't，填在橫線上。

speak   understand   store   walk

> 不管是表達肯定或否定的意思，所有情態動詞後面都連接原形動詞。

1. I _____ the book. It's too difficult.

2. Grandpa _____ because of old age.

3. A computer _____ lots of information.

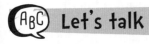 **Let's talk**

Do you have any skills or abilities? Talk about them.

你有哪些技能或能力嗎？請說一說。

I can _____ (e.g. *play the violin*).

Grammar item **59** | ## Use *can* for requests or permission
用 can 表示請求或許可

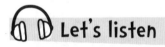 **Let's listen**

Boy: Hey, can you do me a favor?

Lady: Sure.

Boy: Can you watch my stuff for me for a few minutes? I want to go there and have a look. I'll be right back.

Lady: Do you have a ticket? You cannot go in without a ticket.

英文能力 UP！

Can you do me a favor? 用作請求對方幫忙，一般可回答 Sure. 或 Absolutely.（當然可以。）；如果未必能幫忙，可以回答 Depends. What is it?（視乎情況，有什麼要幫忙？）如果幫不上忙，就說句 I'm sorry.（不好意思。）

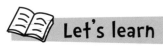 **Let's learn**

We often use *Can you...?* when we ask someone to do something. To ask for permission you can say *Can I...?* To give permission, we use *You can*.

我們會用 Can you...? 來請求別人幫忙，用 Can I...? 來請示別人允許，或用 You can 來表示允許別人做某件事情。

Usage 用法	Examples 例句
Requests 請求	**Can you** pass me the sugar, please? 可以把糖遞過來嗎？
Ask for permission 請示	**Can I** come in now? 我現在可以進來嗎？
Give permission (or not) 許可／不許可	**You can / cannot** go home now. 你現在可以（不可以）回家。

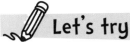 **Let's try**

Write sentences using **can**.

請根據提示，利用 can 造句，然後填在橫線上。

1. Ask for permission: borrow your pen

_____

2. Give permission: go if you like

_____

 Let's talk

What do they say? Act them.

請扮演圖中的人物，說一說他們的對話。

1.

2.

Let's talk 答案：1. Can you lift it up for me, please? 2. You cannot step on the grass.

Let's try 答案：1. Can I borrow your pen? 2. You can go if you like.

131

Grammar item **60** | **Use *could* to talk about past ability**
用 could 表示過去的能力

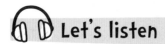 **Let's listen**

Girl: Whose piles of championship medals are these?

Boy: They are my grandpa's. Grandpa was an athlete. He can't run very fast now but when he was young, he could run 100 meters in 11 seconds. He could also swim from one side of the harbor to the other.

Girl: That's brilliant! Does your grandpa do any sports now?

Boy: Yes, he still does weightlifting every day.

英文能力 UP！

could 可以用 was / were able to 來替代，例如 He could swim very fast.（他以前游得很快。）可以說成 He was able to swim very fast.

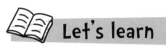

Let's learn

We use *could* to describe abilities in the past.

說明過去我們擁有的能力或會做的事情時，可用 could 來描述。

	Usage 用法	Examples 例句
Past ability 過去的能力	**could** 過去能夠	Mom **could** dance very well when she was young. 媽媽小時候擅長跳舞。
	could not / couldn't 過去不能	I **could not** play the piano back then. 那時候我還不懂彈琴。
Past tense form of *can* can 的過去式	**could / couldn't** 能 / 不能	It was difficult. I **couldn't** understand at all. 那個很難，我完全不明白。

Let's try

Fill in the blanks with **could** or **couldn't**.

請在橫線上填上 could 或 couldn't。

1. I looked everywhere for my pencil but I _____ find it.

2. Grandma _____ look after herself when she was younger.

3. When we went into the room, we _____ smell something burning.

Let's talk

What could your parents do when they were young?
Ask them.

你父母年輕的時候會做些什麼呢？請用以下句式問一問他們。

Could you _____ (e.g. *swim*) when you were young?

Grammar item **61** | **Use *could* for requests and permission**
用 could 表示請求和請示

 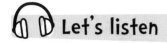 **Let's listen**

Girl: Excuse me, I wonder if you could help me?

Woman: Yes, I can. What happened?

Girl: My dog's gone missing. I can't find it. Do you think you could help me find it? Or could you tell me how to get to the police station so I can ask them for help?

Woman: Calm down first. Let's figure this thing out together.

英文能力 UP！

向別人求助時，我們可以說 Excuse me, I wonder if you could help me?（不好意思，你可以幫幫我嗎？）通常會先說 Excuse me，那是因為會打擾到對方，說了才提出請求比較有禮貌。

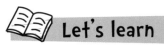
could, like can, is used to ask someone to do something. It is used when you want the request to sound more polite and formal.

could 與 can 一樣，可用來請求別人幫忙，或請示別人允許。但相對 can 來說，could 表現的語氣更有禮貌，會在較正式的場合使用。

Usage 用法	Examples 例句
Requests 請求	Could you open the door, please? 可以請你開門嗎？
	I wonder if you could help me? 你可以幫幫我嗎？
Ask for permission 請示	Could I have more ice cream? 可以多要一點雪糕嗎？
	Could I have a glass of water, please? 我可以喝杯水嗎？

Let's try

Fill in the blanks with the correct verbs.

請在橫線上填上正確的動詞。

1. "Could I u _ _ your telephone?"   "Yes, of course."

2. "Do you think I could _ o _ _ _ _ your bicycle?"
   "Yes, help yourself."

Let's talk

Wouldn't it be fun for your parents to be children and make a request of you? Play this game.

請向你父母提出請求，讓他們做動作，一起玩指令遊戲吧。

Could you _____ (e.g. *sit down*), please?

Yes, certainly. / Yes, of course. / Sure.

Let's try 答案：1. use 2. borrow

Grammar item 62 | Use *may* to ask for permission
用 may 表示請示或許可

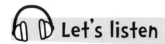

Girl: Mrs. Jones, may I join the school choir, please?

Teacher: Yes, as long as your parents say it's okay. We accept just about anyone interested in music and singing.

Girl: I asked Mom already. She said okay. And I do really love singing.

Teacher: All right. You may join us.

英文能力 UP！

May I...? 是一種客氣的請求，例如在餐廳點餐時，我們可以對服務員說 May I have the menu, please?（可以給我餐牌嗎？）結賬時則可以說 May I have the bill, please?（請結賬。）

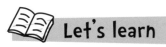 **Let's learn**

We use *May I...?* or *May we...?* to ask for permission politely, and use *may* to show permission.

我們用 May I...? 或 May we...? 來禮貌地請示別人，而 may 也可用來表示允許別人做某件事情。

Usage 用法	Examples 例句
Ask for permission 請示	**May I / we** go home, please? 請問我/我們可以回家了嗎？
Give permission (or not) 許可 / 不許可	**You may** sit down or stand, just as you wish. 你可以坐着也可以站着，請自便。

 **Let's try**

Tick the correct boxes.

請在適當的空格內填 ✓。

當我們提出正式的要求時，用 could 來發問比 may 更有禮貌啊！

	請示	許可
1. May I go to the washroom?	☐	☐
2. You may leave the room now.	☐	☐
3. May I use your computer for a few minutes?	☐	☐

 Let's talk

Let's play 'You may do it now'. Have your mom ask you to do something. If the permission starts with 'You may', you have to do it. If it doesn't start with 'You may' and you do it, you're out.

請和媽媽玩「你可以做」遊戲吧！如果她以 You may 說出指令，你必須按指令做動作；如果媽媽沒有說 You may，你就不能做動作。做錯了便算輸啊！

You may sit down. (*You must sit down*)
Sit down. (*You must not sit down*)

Grammar
item **63** | Use *may / might* to show possibility
用 may / might 表示可能

 Let's listen

Boy:　Do you know if Anna is in the library?

Girl:　I'm not sure. She may not be in the library. She might be having lunch at the canteen now. What's up?

Boy:　I'm going to the art exhibit now. Do you know if Anna wants to go as well?

Girl:　She likes art. She may want to go.

英文能力 UP !

may 和 might 用於推測，説話者並不確定所説的話是否真確，有時候我們可以用 perhaps（也許）來替代，例如 She may want to go.（她可能會去。）可以説成 Perhaps she wants to go.

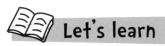 **Let's learn**

We use *may* or *might* to say that something is possible.
There is no important difference between *may* and *might*.

我們會用 may 和 might 來表示有可能發生的事情，兩個單詞的意思大致相同。

Usage 用法		Examples 例句
Positives 肯定句	**may / might** 可能	Anna **may / might** be in the library. 安娜可能在圖書館裏。
		Ask George. He **may / might** know. 問問佐治吧，他可能會知道。
Negatives 否定句	**may / might not** 不可能	Mr. Smith **may / might not** be in his office. 史密夫先生可能不在辦公室。
		He **may / might not** come to the party tonight. 他可能不來參加今晚的派對。

 **Let's try**

Circle the correct answers.

請把正確的答案圈出來。

> 除了 might 是 may 的過去式時，may 和 might 一般可互相替換。

1. She (may be / might) having dinner.

2. They (may be go / might go) to America for holiday.

3. I want to buy this, but I (may not have / might have) enough money.

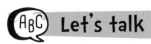 **Let's talk**

Can you solve this riddle? Talk about it with your friends.

你能猜出這道謎題嗎？請考一考你的朋友。

It has hands, but it can't scratch itself.

It might be a
_____ .

Grammar item 64 | Use *will / would* for requests, offers or invitations
用 will / would 來請求、建議或邀請

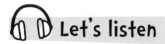 Let's listen

Boy: Will you show me how to play the violin?

Girl: Okay, I will tell you what to do. Stand with a straight back. Hold the violin.

Boy: Like this? It's so cool. Do I look like a musician? You know, I would like to be a famous musician when I grow up.

Girl: Oh stop, stop! Would you please stop making that noise!

英文能力 UP！

大家看到 will 的時候，通常都會馬上反應這是「將來式」，但其實它還可以用來表示請求的呢。

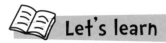 **Let's learn**

We use *will* or *would* when we ask someone to do something.
We use *Would you like…?* to make offers or give invitations.

我們用 will 或 would 來請求別人幫忙，還會用 Would you like...?
來建議或邀請。

Usage 用法	Examples 例句
Requests 一般的請求	Shut the windows, **will you**? 可以把窗戶關上嗎？
Polite requests 客氣的請求	**Would** you shut the windows, please? 請把窗戶關上好嗎？
Offers and invitations 建議或邀請	**Would you like** something to drink? 你要喝些什麼飲料嗎？

 **Let's try**

Write sentences using **will** or **would**.

請根據提示，利用 will 或 would 造句，然後填在橫線上。

1. Polite request: shut the door

> Would you 是比 Will you 更鄭重 的表達方式。

_____

2. Invitation: go to a movie tonight

_____

 Let's talk

Imagine you are a waiter / waitress and your parents are
customers. Take their orders.

請利用以下句式扮演餐廳服務員，替你父母點餐，說出對話。

Would you like _____ (e.g. *some soup*)?

Yes, I would. / That sounds great.
No, I wouldn't. / No, thanks.

Let's try 答案：1. Would you shut the door, please? 2. Would you like to go to a movie tonight?

Grammar item **65** | **Use *must* to express an obligation**
用 must 表示必須

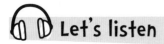 **Let's listen**

Girl: We must hurry, or we'll miss the train.

Boy: You go ahead with them. I have lost my cap and I have to find it.

Girl: Hurry up! It's late. We mustn't miss the train, or we'll have to wait another hour.

Boy: Ok, just give me five minutes.

英文能力 UP！

must 通常可用 have to 來取代，例如 We must hurry.（我們要趕快一點。）可以説成 We have to hurry.

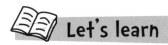 **Let's learn**

We use *must* to talk about rules. For the negatives, we can use *must not* or *mustn't*.

我們會用 must 來説「必須」做的事情，表示否定的意思時用 must not 或 mustn't。

Usage 用法		Examples 例句
Positives 肯定句	**must** 必須	You **must** keep quiet in the library. 你在圖書館必須安靜一些。
		It's seven o'clock. I **must** go now. 七點鐘了，我現在得走。
Negatives 否定句	**must not / mustn't** 絕不能	I **must not** play on the road. 我絕不能在馬路上玩耍。
		You **mustn't** tell anyone what I said. 你千萬不能把我説的話告訴別人。

 **Let's try**

Correct the sentences.

請改正句子，然後填在橫線上。

1. We mustn't late for school.

_____

2. You must to work harder if you want to pass the exam.

_____

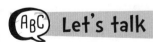 **Let's talk**

What are the safety rules for children at home? Talk about it.

孩子在家裏要遵守什麼安全規則呢？請説一説。

 I must not / mustn't _____ (e.g. *open the door to a stranger*).

Grammar item **66** | **Use *ought to / should* for advice**
用 ought to / should 提出建議

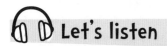

Boy: I don't feel well. Should I go to see the doctor?

Girl: You were eating more than you should. Your belly expands as big as a balloon now.

Boy: What should I do?

Girl: You shouldn't eat too much from now on. You should eat plenty of vegetables and fruit to stay healthy. You also ought to take plenty of exercise.

英文能力 UP！

在疑問句中，should 用來徵求別人的建議，例如 What should I do?（我該怎麼辦？）或 Should I trust her?（我應該相信她嗎？）

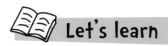 **Let's learn**

We use *ought to* or *should* to give or ask for advice. For the negatives, we can use *ought not to*, *should not* or *shouldn't*.

我們會用 should 或 ought to 來建議「應該」做的事情，表示否定的意思時用 should not / shouldn't 或 ought not to。

Usage 用法		Examples 例句
Positives 肯定句	should 或 ought to 應該	We **should** respect our teachers. 我們應該尊敬老師。 I **ought to** eat more vegetables. 我應該多吃點蔬菜。
Negatives 否定句	should not / shouldn't 或 ought not to 不應	They **should not** shout in the classroom. 他們不應在課室裏大叫。 You **ought not to** miss the play. 你不應錯過那齣話劇。

 **Let's try**

Correct the sentences.

請改正句子，然後填在橫線上。

句子中的 ought to 和 should 可互相替換，但 ought to 語氣稍重。

1. I ought to doing more exercise.

_____

2. You shouldn't ate too much junk food.

_____

(ABC) **Let's talk**

How should children behave in these places? Talk about it.

我們在這些地方需要遵守什麼規則呢？請説一説。

✿ Park　　　✿ Restaurant　　　✿ Cinema

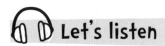 **Let's listen**

Girl: Shall we finish our homework today?

Boy: No, we don't have to do it today. We can do it on the weekend. Today is a holiday so let's do something fun instead.

Girl: Shall we go ice skating? Will you teach me how to skate?

Boy: I'm not good at ice skating. You should take lessons from a proper coach. Shall we go to a movie instead?

英文能力 UP！

Shall we go to a movie?（我們去看電影好嗎？）是美式說法，英式
英語的說法是 Shall we go to the cinema?

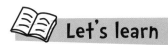 **Let's learn**

Shall I...? or *Shall we...?* is used to make offers and suggestions politely. We use *shall* to ask for advice, too.

我們用 Shall I...? 和 Shall we...? 有禮地提出建議，還會用 shall 來詢問別人的意見。

Usage 用法	Examples 例句
Suggestions 提出建議	**Shall I** carry this for you? 我幫你拿這個吧？ **Shall we** go swimming? 我們去游泳吧？
Ask for advice 詢問意見	**What shall I / we** get for dinner? 晚飯我/我們該做什麼來吃？

 **Let's try**

Fill in the blanks with the correct words.

請根據提示，在橫線上填上正確的答案。

1. (Ask for advice) _____ _____ _____ bring to the picnic?

2. (Suggestion) _____ _____ help you with the housework?

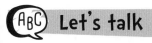 **Let's talk**

Read out and sing this nursery rhyme.

請朗讀這首兒歌一遍，然後唱出來。

> One, two, what shall we do?
> Three, four, measure and pour.
> Five, six, whisk and mix.
> Seven, eight, bake the cake.
> Nine, ten, in the oven.

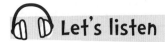 **Let's listen**

Boy:　This temple now stands completely deserted. Come on, let's see what's inside.

Girl:　No, I dare not. This place looks bizarre. 古怪

Boy:　OK, wait for me here. I'll go inside.

Girl:　No! How dare you leave me alone here? We'd better leave. Come with me. I dare not walk home alone.

英文能力 UP！

dare 本來是動詞，但當它用作情態動詞時，就不會有任何時態或形式變化，後面也可直接加上原形動詞。例如我們説 She dare not do that.（她不敢做那件事。），而不説 She dares not do that.

148

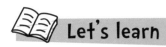 **Let's learn**

dare means to be brave enough to do something. It is usually used in negative sentences and some special expressions.

dare 表示敢於做危險或害怕的事情，一般用於否定句或某些特別情況。

Usage 用法		Examples 例句
Negatives 否定句	**dare not / daren't** （不敢做某件事情）	I **daren't** tell Mom that I've lost the money. 我不敢告訴媽媽我把錢弄丟了。 She **daren't** tell Dad what she thinks. 她不敢把自己的想法告訴爸爸。
Special expressions 特別情況	• **Dare…! / ?** • **How dare…! / ?** （竟敢、膽敢，表示語氣憤怒或震驚）	**How dare** you talk to the teacher like that? 你膽敢這樣跟老師說話？ **Dare** you shout at your parents like that! 你竟敢這樣呼喝父母！

 **Let's try**

Fill in the blanks with the correct words.

請根據提示，在橫線上填上正確的答案。

1. She is so afraid that she _____ _____ move.

2. _____ _____ he take my bicycle without even asking!

(ABC) **Let's talk**

Truth or dare? Play the game with your friends.

請利用以下句式，跟你朋友玩「真心話大冒險」遊戲吧。

Truth: Tell me the truth, _____ (e.g. *dare you go into a haunted house*)?

Dare: (e.g. *Act like a monkey.*) Dare you do it?

Let's try 答案：1. dare not　2. How dare

> Grammar item **69** | **Use *used to* for past habits and situations**
> 用 used to 表示過去的習慣和狀況

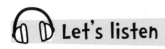 **Let's listen**

Boy: Do you go swimming very often?

Girl: Not now, but I used to. I used to swim a lot when I was younger. Do you see the villas over there?

Boy: Yes, they look very high-class.

Girl: There used to be a beach over there and sometimes you could see dolphins jumping out of the water. But they're all gone now.

英文能力 UP！

I used to swim a lot.（我以前常常游泳。）不能説成 I use to swim a lot. 或 I was used to swim a lot. 但在問句形式就可説 Did you use to swim a lot?（你以前經常游泳嗎？）

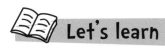 **Let's learn**

We use *used to* to say that something regularly happened in the past but no longer happens. We also use *used to* for past situations which no longer exist.

我們用 used to 來說以前經常做的事或過去的狀況，而這些事情現在已不存在了。

Usage 用法	Examples 例句
Past habits 以前經常做的事	Mr. Smith **used to** smoke. 史密夫先生以前會抽煙。
	I **used to** eat chocolate a lot. 我以前經常吃很多巧克力。
Past situations 過去的狀況	She **used to** be fat. 她以前很胖。
	They **used to** live in a small village. 他們以前住在一條小村莊裏。

 **Let's try**

Complete the sentences with **used to**.

請根據提示，利用 used to 完成句子，填在橫線上。

1. Anna _____ long hair but she got it cut some time ago.

2. There _____ an old temple here, but they knocked it down.

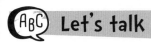 **Let's talk**

Did you have any bad habits when you were younger that you don't have now? Talk about it.

你以前有些什麼壞習慣嗎？請說一說。

I used to _____ (e.g. *cry a lot*), but I don't do it anymore.

Let's try 答案：1. used to have   2. used to be

151

Grammar item **70** | **Indefinite pronouns - People**
不定代名詞：人物

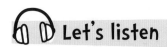 Let's listen

Girl: Somebody is at the door. Can you check who it is, please?

Boy: Nobody is here. There isn't anybody here at all. But someone left a parcel behind. Should we open it?

Girl: No! That's really strange, don't you think so? Shouldn't we ask somebody to help?

Boy: Everybody has already left. No one is going to help us.

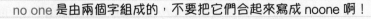

英文能力 UP！

no one 是由兩個字組成的，不要把它們合起來寫成 noone 啊！

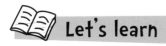 **Let's learn**

We use *somebody*, *anybody*, *nobody* or *everybody* to refer to people in a general way.

當我們不清楚要説的人是誰或具體的人數時，就可以用 somebody、anybody、nobody 或 everybody。

Usage 用法		Examples 例句
somebody / someone 某人	**Positives & Questions** 肯定句和疑問句	**Somebody** is in the classroom. 有人在課室裏。
anybody / anyone 任何人	**Negatives & Questions** 否定句和疑問句	Is there **anyone** in the classroom? 課室裏有人嗎？
nobody / no one 沒有人	**Negatives** 否定句	There is **nobody** in the classroom. 課室裏沒有人。
everybody / everyone 每個人	**Positives & Questions** 肯定句和疑問句	**Everyone** is in the classroom. 所有人都在課室裏。

 **Let's try**

Fill in the blanks with indefinite pronouns.

請在橫線上填上正確的不定代名詞。

1. Does _____ know the answer?

2. _____ believed him. He's a liar.

> 在口語中，somebody、anybody、nobody 比 someone、anyone、no one 更常用。

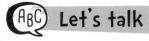 **Let's talk**

If you could be someone else, would you? Talk about it.

如果你能變成另外一個人，你會變成誰？請説一説。

> If I could be someone else, I would be _____.
> It's because _____.

Let's try 答案：1. anybody / anyone   2. Nobody / No one

Grammar item 71	**Indefinite pronouns - Things** 不定代名詞：事物

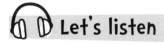 **Let's listen**

Boy: I found this treasure chest on the ground. But there isn't anything left – nothing at all, someone took it all.

Girl: There's something about this place that frightens me. Everything looks so strange.

Boy: Let's explore this place. There might be hidden treasure.

Girl: Argh! Something just crawled over my shoulder! Let's go! We're falling behind!

英文能力 UP！

雖然 everything 指「所有東西」，但後面必須連接表示單數的動詞，例如 Everything is ready.（一切就緒。）、Everything looks so strange.（一切看來都很奇怪。）

154

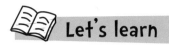 **Let's learn**

We use *something*, *anything*, *nothing* or *everything*
to refer to things in a general way.
當我們不清楚要說的東西是什麼或具體的數量時，就可以用
something、anything、nothing 或 everything。

Usage 用法		Examples 例句
something 某些東西	**Positives & Questions** 肯定句和疑問句	I'm hungry. I'd like **something** to eat. 我餓了，我想吃東西。
anything 任何東西	**Negatives & Questions** 否定句和疑問句	I don't want **anything** from this shop. 我沒有什麼要在這商店買。
nothing 沒有東西	**Negatives** 否定句	I have **nothing** to do today. 我今天沒事做。
everything 所有東西	**Positives & Questions** 肯定句和疑問句	Why is **everything** so expensive here? 為什麼這裏的東西這麼貴？

 **Let's try**

Fill in the blanks with indefinite pronouns.
請在橫線上填上正確的不定代名詞。

1. The poor dog doesn't have _____ to eat.

2. Do you have _____ you need for the picnic?

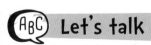 **Let's talk**

Ask your parents to guess what you're holding in your hand.
請找一些小物件放進手中，然後讓你父母猜猜那是什麼吧。

> I'm holding something (e.g. *a coin*) in my hand.
> Guess what it is?

Grammar item **72** | **Indefinite pronouns - Places** 不定代名詞：地方

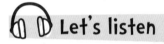

Boy: Oh, what's that little creature? Is it a kitten?

Girl: Hush! Keep your voice down. It's my new pet. It's called Milly.

Boy: Where did you get it from?

Girl: I was walking home yesterday. Somewhere on the street I heard something squeaking. I looked around everywhere but it seemed to be coming from nowhere. Then, I found it somewhere near the lake. It's so cute, isn't it?

英文能力 UP！

在美式英語中，everywhere 也可說成 everyplace，例如 We see them everyplace we go.（我們到哪裏都看到他們。）

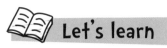

Let's learn

We use *somewhere*, *anywhere*, *nowhere* or *everywhere* to refer to places in a general way.

當我們不清楚要説的是什麼地方或具體的地點時，就可以用 somewhere、anywhere、nowhere 或 everywhere。

Usage 用法		Examples 例句
somewhere 某些地方	**Positives & Questions** 肯定句和疑問句	I forgot my pencil case **somewhere**. 我忘了把筆盒放在哪裏。
anywhere 任何地方	**Negatives & Questions** 否定句和疑問句	I can't find it **anywhere**. 我四處也找不到它。
nowhere 沒有地方	**Negatives** 否定句	I have **nowhere** to sit. 我沒有地方坐下。
everywhere 所有地方	**Positives & Questions** 肯定句和疑問句	He wears his cap **everywhere** he goes. 他到哪裏都戴着帽子。

Let's try

Fill in the blanks with indefinite pronouns.

請在橫線上填上正確的不定代名詞。

1. These beggars have _____ to live.

2. Oh no! I forgot my sunglasses _____ .

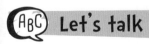

Let's talk

Ask your parents to guess where you've hidden something.

請把一個物件藏在家裏的某個角落，然後讓你父母猜猜放在哪裏吧。

I've hidden _____ (e.g. *my ruler*) somewhere. Guess where it is?

<table>
<tr><td>Grammar item</td><td>73</td><td>Connecting words - and / but / or
連接的詞語</td></tr>
</table>

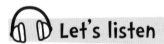 Let's listen

Girl: Anna and I are just going out to have a hamburger. Do you want to come too?

Boy: I'd love to, but I've just had a sandwich actually. Do me a favour. Can you get me some juice?

Girl: Sure. Do you prefer orange or apple juice?

Boy: please. Thanks.
Orange juice 的縮寫

英文能力 UP！

不要說 I and Ann 或 I and my friends，要把 I 放在後面，說成 Ann and I 或 My friends and I，例如 Anna and I went to school together. （我和安娜一起上學。）

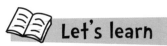 **Let's learn**

Conjuctions, such as *and*, *but* and *or*, join ideas in sentences together.

連接詞 and、but 和 or 能把句中的意思連接起來。

Usage 用法	Examples 例句
A and B 和/然後 （連接相同部分）	Anna **and** Joey are sisters. 安娜和祖兒是姊妹。 He brushed his teeth **and** went to bed. 他刷牙，然後睡覺。
A but B 但是 （表示相反的意思）	The food here is nice **but** expensive. 這裏的食物不錯，但是貴了點。 He can play the piano, **but** he can't play the violin. 他會彈琴，但不會拉小提琴。
A or B 或 （表示兩項中 選一項）	Which do you like, rice **or** noodles? 你想要哪一個，米飯或麵條？ Do you like to go swimming **or** play badminton? 你想去游泳還是打羽毛球？

 **Let's try**

Fill in the blanks with the correct conjunctions.

請在橫線上填上正確的連接詞。

1. Thomas is kind _____ helpful.

2. You can have bread, salad, _____ soup.

(ABC) **Let's talk**

What shall we do on the weekend? Give some suggestions to your parents.

這周末有些什麼活動呢？請給你父母提供一些建議吧。

Shall we _____ or _____
(e.g. *go to a movie* or *stay at home*) ?

Grammar item **74**

Connecting words - because / so / although / if / unless
連接的詞語

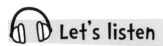 Let's listen

Boy: Do you want to watch that movie?

Girl: No, I can't watch that movie because I'll have a bad dream. If I watch something scary, I'll get nightmares.

Boy: This is just a children's movie, so I don't think you'll get scared.

Girl: Although it's a children movie, I should avoid it unless there're no vampires in it.

英文能力 UP！

although 和 but 不能共用，只能二選其一，我們可以說 It's cheap, but it's very good. 或 Although it's cheap, it's very good.（它雖是便宜貨，但很好。）

160

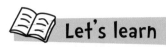 **Let's learn**

because talks about a cause and *so* tells you the result. *although* tells something surprising, and *if* and *unless* are used to make a condition.

because 説出原因，so 交代結果。although 説出令人意外的事情；if 和 unless 用來帶出條件。

Usage 用法	Examples 例句
結果 **because** 原因	I wore my raincoat **because** it was raining. 我穿雨衣是因為下雨。
原因 **so** 結果	It was raining **so** I wore my raincoat. 下雨了，所以我穿了雨衣。
Although...意外的結果	**Although** it was raining, I didn't wear my raincoat. 雖然下雨，但是我不穿雨衣。
結果 **if** 條件	I will wear my raincoat **if** it rains. 如果下雨，我就會穿雨衣。
結果 **unless** 條件	I won't wear my raincoat **unless** it rains. 除非下雨，否則我不會穿雨衣。

 **Let's try**

Fill in the blanks with the correct conjunctions.

請在橫線上填上正確的連接詞。

1. You will not succeed _____ you work hard.

2. It's very late, _____ we'd better go home now.

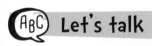 **Let's talk**

Use **although** to tell something surprising about yourself.

你會做一些令人意想不到的事情嗎？請用以下句式説一説。

Although I'm a kid, I _____.

Grammar item **75** | **Connecting words - before / after / when / until**
連接的詞語

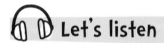 **Let's listen**

Boy: Hello, I'm going grocery shopping with Mom. You (wanna) come?

want to 的
口語用法

Girl: I can go with you after I finish my homework.

Boy: Ok. I'll wait until you finish your homework. Mom asked me to make a list before we go. She said making a list would save us time once we are there.

Girl: OK, I'll join you when I'm done with my homework.

英文能力 UP！

用 until 連接的句子，一般會用將來式，例如 We will wait until the rain stops. （我們會等到雨停為止。）

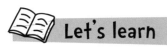 **Let's learn**

before and *after* answer questions about the sequence of events. *when* answers questions about time. *until* indicates when something will end.

before 和 after 説明事情發生的先後順序；when 説明事情發生的時間；until 能指出事情終結的時間。

Usage 用法	Examples 例句
before 在……之前	I must leave **before** it gets dark. 在天黑以前，我必須離開。
after 在……之後	I will go home **after** I finish my homework. 我做完功課就會回家了。
when 當……的時候	The dog jumped up **when** it saw me. 當那隻狗見到我就跳了起來。
until 直到……為止	I will wait here **until** Mom comes. 我會在這裏等，直至媽媽來到。

 **Let's try**

Fill in the blanks with the correct conjunctions.
請在橫線上填上正確的連接詞。

> until 的末尾只一個 l，千萬不要拼寫成 untill 啊！

1. _____ I wash my hands, I dry them.

2. I will not go out _____ I hear from you.

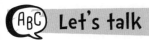 **Let's talk**

What is your daily routine? Talk about it.
你平常的早上是怎麼過的呢？請利用以下提示説一説。

- ✿ Wake up
- ✿ Get dressed
- ✿ Brush teeth
- ✿ Eat breakfast

I usually _____ before / after _____.

Grammar item 76 | **Connecting words in pairs** 成對使用的連接詞

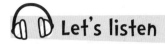 **Let's listen**

Girl: What's the best way of getting to the airport?

Boy: Well, you can take either the airport bus or the express train. Both the bus and the train will take you to the airport in less than an hour. The train is fast but expensive. The bus is not only fast but also cheap.

Girl: Can I take the ferry or the minibus?

Boy: No, neither the ferry nor the minibus goes to the airport.

英文能力UP！

在 either A or B 或 neither A nor B 的句式中，如果 A 和 B 都是單數，後面就要連接表示單數的動詞，例如 Either the bus or the train goes to the airport. 但 A 或 B 其中一個是複數時，動詞就要跟它最接近的事物互相對應，例如 Either the train or the buses go to the airport.

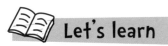 **Let's learn**

Some connectiong words always show up in pairs.

有些連接詞必須一對地使用，兩個單詞是不能分開的。

Usage 用法	Examples 例句	Anna	Joey
either A or B 不是 A，就是 B	You can invite **either** Anna **or** Joey. 你只能邀請安娜或祖兒。	✓	✗
		✗	✓
neither A nor B 既不是 A，也不是 A	**Neither** Anna **nor** Joey came. 安娜和祖兒都沒有來。	✗	✗
both A and B A 和 B 都是	**Both** Anna **and** Joey came. 安娜和祖兒兩個都來了。	✓	✓
not only A but also B 不僅是 A，而且是 B	**Not only** Anna **but also** Joey came. 不僅安娜來了，而且祖兒也來了。	✓	✓

 **Let's try**

Fill in the blanks with the correct connecting words.

請在橫線上填上正確的連接詞。

1. You can have ＿＿＿＿＿＿ Cola or juice.

2. ＿＿＿＿＿＿ Grandma nor Grandpa speaks English.

3. Exercise is good for ＿＿＿＿＿＿ the body and the mind.

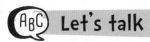 **Let's talk**

What instruments can you play or what languages can you speak? Talk about it.

你能玩哪些樂器，又會説哪些語言呢？請説一説。

 I can play / speak either ＿＿＿＿ or ＿＿＿＿ .

Let's try 答案：1. either　2. Neither　3. both

Grammar item **77** | **Adverbs of manner**
狀態副詞

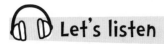 **Let's listen**

Girl: Where can we hide so that they can't find us?

Boy: Hush, hush! Speak softly. I know a secret place. Come with me. But we have to walk very slowly and silently.

Girl: Okay. I'll follow you.

Boy: Do you see the cave over there? Once we get to the open area, we'll have to run quickly to the cave. We'll be safe there.

英文能力 UP！

不少副詞都是以 -ly 結尾，但有些單詞的末尾雖然是 -ly，卻不是副詞，

而是形容詞，例如 ugly、friendly、lovely、lonely。

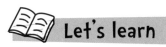 **Let's learn**

Adverbs of manner are used to describe 'how' the action happens. They usually follow the verbs.

狀態副詞告訴我們事情或動作是如何發生的，它通常放在動詞後面。

Rules 規則			Examples 例句
在形容詞後面加上 -ly 或 -ily	**quick** **greedy**	→ **quickly** → **greedily**	He ran home quick**ly**. 他匆匆地跑回家裏。
			The lion ate its food greed**ily**. 獅子貪婪地把食物吃掉。
不規則變化	**well、hard、fast** （不要寫成 hardly、fastly）		She sings well. 她歌唱得很好。
			He works hard. 他努力地工作。

 **Let's try**

Circle the adverbs in the sentences.

請把句中的副詞圈出來。

1. He is a friendly athlete. He also runs fast.

2. This lovely baby boy sometimes cries loudly.

3. That lonely old man often walks slowly and quietly in the park.

 Let's talk

What is something you can do easily? Talk about it.

哪些事情對你來說是輕而易舉的呢？請説一説。

> I can _____ (e.g. *fly a kite*) easily.

Let's try 答案：1. fast　2. loudly　3. slowly; quietly

Grammar item **78** | **Adverbs of frequency**
頻率副詞

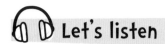 Let's listen

Girl: What is something you usually do on Sunday?

Boy: I usually go to church with Mom and Dad on Sunday. We sometimes go to a dim sum restaurant, and we sometimes watch a movie. What about you? Where do you often go on weekends?

Girl: I never go to church, but I often go to my cousin's house. I always have a good time!

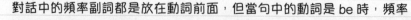

英文能力 UP！

對話中的頻率副詞都是放在動詞前面，但當句中的動詞是 be 時，頻率副詞就會改為放在後面，例如 I am always happy.（我總是很快樂。）

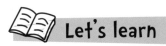 **Let's learn**

Adverbs of frequency are used to say 'how often' things happen.

我們用頻率副詞來表示事情或動作發生的次數多或少。

Frequency 發生頻率 100%	always 總是	I **always** take the school bus to school. 我總是坐校巴上學。
	usually 通常	Mom **usually** goes jogging on Sunday. 媽媽通常在星期天去緩步跑。
	often 常常	Dad **often** has pudding for dessert. 爸爸常常吃布丁做甜品。
	sometimes 有時候	We **sometimes** go to the seashore. 我們有時候會去海邊。
	seldom 很少	He **seldom** does exercise. 他很少做運動。
0%	never 從不	Justin **never** fails in an exam. 賈斯丁考試從不曾不及格。

 **Let's try**

Fill in the blanks with the correct words.

請根據提示，在橫線上填上正確的答案。

1. Justin _____ (sometimes / be) late for school.

2. You must _____ (always / fasten) your seat belt.

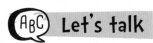 **Let's talk**

What is something a pupil should never do in class? Talk about it.

在課室內，學生絕不能做哪些行為呢？請說一說。

A pupil should never _____ (e.g. *fall asleep*) in class.

Grammar
item **79** | **Adverbs of degree**
程度副詞

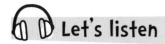 **Let's listen**

Girl: I'm quite nervous about the exam tomorrow.

Boy: Why are you so nervous? You're always a very good student. And you did extremely well in the last exam.

Girl: I got sick last week. I didn't have enough time to prepare for the exam. I'm really worried.

Boy: Don't worry, you'll be fine.

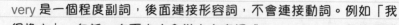

英文能力 UP！

very 是一個程度副詞，後面連接形容詞，不會連接動詞。例如「我很擔心」一句話，有不少人會從中文直譯成 I very worry. 但這是錯的，應說成 I'm very worried.

170

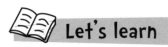 **Let's learn**

Adverbs of degree are used to describe the degree or extent that the action happens.

我們用程度副詞來使詞語的意思變得更強烈或更微弱。

Degree 強弱程度 最強 ↓ 最弱	extremely 極度	She plays the violin **extremely** well. 她的小提琴拉得極好。
	very 非常 really 真的	This cake is **very / really** nice. 這蛋糕真好吃。
	too 太 quite 相當 so 很	The music is **too** loud. 音樂太大聲了。 The movie is **quite** interesting. 那電影頗有趣。 She is **so** clever. 她很聰明。
	slightly 稍微	He is **slightly** overweight. 他有少許過胖。
	hardly 幾乎不	It is **hardly** visible. 幾乎看不見。

 **Let's try**

Fill in the blanks with the correct adverbs.

請在橫線上填上正確的副詞。

1. You've put _____ much salt into the soup.

2. It's a _____ different color. Can you see the difference?

(ABC) **Let's talk**

How do you feel today? Use the adverbs of degree to talk about it.

你今天的心情怎麼樣呢？請用程度副詞來説一説。

I feel _____ (e.g. *extremely good*) today.

Grammar item 80 | Adverbs of time 時間副詞

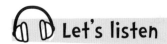

Boy: You're not going to the school picnic tomorrow?

Girl: No, I just moved into my new house yesterday. I need to help Mom and Dad unpack this week.

Boy: You're going to change schools soon, aren't you?

Girl: Yes, I'll switch to a school which is closer to my new home, but not this year. Maybe next year. Well, I've got to go now. Talk to you later.

英文能力 UP！

在 last、this、next、yesterday、today、tomorrow 前面不用加任何單詞連接句子，例如 I'll see you (✗ on) next Monday.（下周一見。）、They went to Japan (✗ in) last summer.（他們在去年夏天到日本去。）

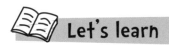 **Let's learn**

Adverbs of time tell us when an action happened.
時間副詞指出事情或動作在什麼時候發生。

just 剛剛	I **just** went swimming. 我剛剛去了游泳。
now 現在	Let's go there **now**. 我們現在就去那裏。
soon 快要、馬上	I will leave **soon**. 我馬上會離開了。
later 晚一點	I will call you **later**. 我晚一點給你打電話。
last 上個　**week** 星期 **this** 這個 ＋ **month** 月 **next** 下個　（或其他時間）	We had barbecue dinner **last night**. 我們昨晚燒烤來做晚餐。
yesterday / today / tomorrow 昨天、今天、明天	I went there **yesterday**. 我昨天去了。 See you **tomorrow**. 明天見。

 **Let's try**

Circle the correct adverbs.
請把正確的副詞圈出來。

> 時間副詞一般放在
> 句末或句子中間，
> 但有時會放在句子
> 開首作強調。

1. He was (just / soon / later) leaving when the phone rang.

2. I'm going out for a bit — I'll see you (now / today / later).

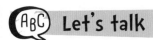 **Let's talk**

Make a 'Paper Fortune Teller' and write down
8 activities, then play with your parents.
請在網上找「東南西北摺紙遊戲」的製作方法，並在內
側寫上 8 個活動，然後用以下句式跟你父母玩一玩。

> What shall we do now / tonight / etc. ?

> Let's ＿＿＿＿＿＿ (*read the hidden message*).

Grammar item **81** | **Adverbs of place**
地方副詞

 Let's listen

Boy: What are you doing upstairs?

Girl: I'm looking for my cat. I searched everywhere I could think of, but it's nowhere to be found. Can you help me look around?

Boy: I think I saw your cat outside an hour ago. She ran away!

Girl: Oh, look! There she is! Come here! Come back to me, Milly!

英文能力 UP！

here 和 there 是最常用的地方副詞，有時會把它們放在句子開頭來加強語氣或發出感歎，例如 Here comes the bus!（巴士來了！）、There it is!（牠在那裏！）

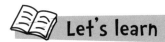 **Let's learn**

Adverbs of place tell us where something happened. They usually follow the verbs, too.

地方副詞一般放在動詞後面，説明事情或動作發生的地點。

in 向裏面 **out** 向外面	Come **in**! Get **out**! 進來吧！出去！
away 遠去 **back** 回來	The dog ran **away**, and then it ran **back**. 小狗跑遠了，然後又跑回來。
here 這裏 **there** 那裏	Stay **here**. I'll go **there**. 待在這兒，我到那邊去。
upstairs 樓上 **downstairs** 樓下	He went **upstairs** / **downstairs** to his room. 他走到樓上 / 樓下去他的房間。
inside 裏面 **outside** 外面	They went **inside** / **outside**. 他們進去了 / 到外面去了。

 **Let's try**

Circle the adverbs in the sentences.

請把句中的副詞圈出來。

> 地方副詞只和動詞搭配，不會跟形容詞或其他副詞連接。

1. It's raining. Let's stay inside.

2. The milk is sour. Throw it away!

3. Dad ran downstairs to answer the phone.

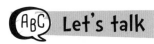 **Let's talk**

Ask your parents to give these instructions. Follow and act them out.

請你父母説出以下指令，讓你跟着指令做這些動作。

Come in / here / downstairs / inside.

Go out / there / upstairs / outside.

Grammar item 82 | **Prepositions of time - at / on / in**
時間介詞

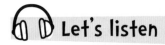

Girl:　When can you bring back those books I lent you? I need to return them to the library in five days.

Boy:　Will you be here on Saturday? I can bring the books back to you then.

Girl:　No, I'll be at home on the weekend. Why don't you drop in at any time on Saturday?

Boy:　Okay, I'll see you on Saturday morning at 10 o'clock.

英文能力 UP！

我們用中文會說「在十點」、「在星期日」、「在冬天」等，但用英文就要分別說成 at 10 o'clock、on Sunday、in winter。

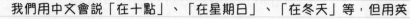

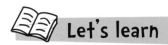

Let's learn

Prepositions of time show the time something happened.

時間介詞用來帶出事情發生的時間,最常用的是 at、on 和 in。

Usage 用法	Examples 例子		
at (a precise time) 帶出確切的 時間或節日	**at** 9 am 在早上九點	**at** sunset 夕陽之際	**at** Christmas 聖誕節期間
on (days or dates) 帶出日期和 特定日子	**on** Tuesday 在星期二	**on** my birthday 我生日的那一天	**on** July 1st 在七月一日
in (a long period) 帶出一段 頗長的時間	**in** August 八月的時候	**in** summer 在夏天	**in** 2019 在二〇一九年

Let's try

Fill in the blanks with the correct prepositions.

請在橫線上填上正確的介詞。

1. My birthday is _____ February 28th.

2. He went to bed _____ midnight and got up _____ seven the next morning.

Let's talk

Let's play "What time do we have snacks, Mr. Fox?" with your parents.

請利用以下句式,跟你父母一起玩玩「狐狸先生吃小食」的遊戲吧。

Players: What time do we have snacks, Mr Fox?

Mr. Fox: At _____ (e.g. 3) o'clock.
           (*Players then take three steps forward*)
           It's snack time!
           (*Players have to run in order not to be caught*)

Grammar item 83 | Prepositions of place - at / on / in
位置介詞

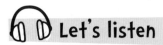 Let's listen

Girl:　There's no one in the classroom. Where've they all gone?

Boy:　Are they playing in the playground?

Girl:　No, I've looked everywhere but I can't find them. Ahh, they might be on the rooftop. I haven't yet searched the rooftop.

Boy:　Hey, look at this notice at the top of the board. No wonder nobody is at school, it's a holiday today.

英文能力 UP！

我們用中文會説「在課室」、「在天台」、「在學校」等，但用英文就要分別説成 in the classroom、on the rooftop、at school。

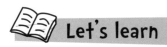 **Let's learn**

We use prepositions of place when we talk about the location of things.

位置介詞用來帶出事物所在的地點，最常用的也是 at、on 和 in。

Usage 用法	Examples 例子		
at (a point) 帶出一點 的位置	**at** the bus stop 在巴士站	**at** home 在家裏	**at** school 在學校
	at the entrance 在入口	**at** the back 在後面	**at** the door 在門前
on (a surface) 帶出平面和比 一點大的空間	**on** page 10 在第十頁	**on** my bed 在我的牀上	**on** the ground 在地上
	on the wall 在牆上	**on** your face 在你的臉上	**on** stage 舞臺上
in (an enclosed space) 帶出圍住或 相對更大的空間	**in** a box 在盒子裏	**in** space 在太空裏	**in** my bedroom 在我的睡房裏
	in the water 在水中	**in** China 在中國	**in** an armchair 在扶手椅裏

 Let's try

Fill in the blanks with the correct prepositions.

請在橫線上填上正確的介詞。

1. What did you learn _____ class today?

2. Aunt Lily lives _____ a small village _____ the north coast.

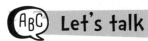 **Let's talk**

Where do you live? Talk about it.

你住在哪裏？請説一説。

I live on the _____ floor at _____
樓層　　　　　　　　　　　街道及街號
in _____ .
城市名

| Grammar item 84 | **More prepositions of place** 其他位置介詞 |

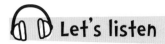

Boy: Where are you, Milly? I can't see you. Are you hiding under the bed?

Girl: No, she's not. She's not there. I think she's behind the cupboard on the right of the TV.

Boy: Yeap, I hear it now! There she is. She's crawling above the cupboard. Yay, I got you, Milly!

Girl: Oh no, she's running away! Catch her!

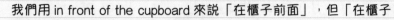

英文能力 UP！

我們用 in front of the cupboard 來說「在櫃子前面」，但「在櫃子後面」可不能說成 behind of the cupboard 啊！

180

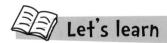 **Let's learn**

These prepositions of place are also used to talk about the location of things.

這些位置介詞也是用來帶出物件所在的地點。

Usage 用法	Examples 例句
in front of / behind 在前面 / 後面	Don't stand **in front of** the TV screen. 不要站在電視屏幕前。 The boy hid himself **behind** the bushes. 男孩躲到樹叢後面去了。
on the right / left 在右面 / 左面	The cinema is **on the right of** the mall. 電影院在商場的右邊。 The boys sit **on the left of** the girls. 男孩坐在女孩左邊。
above / under 在上面 / 下面	The birds are flying **above** the trees. 鳥兒在樹林上飛翔。 We sheltered **under** a tree. 我們躲在樹下。

 **Let's try**

Fill in the blanks with the correct prepositions.

請在橫線上填上正確的介詞。

> right 和 left 同時是形容詞，例如 my left eye、my right arm。

1. The airplane flew _____ the clouds.

2. She has hidden the box _____ the bed.

3. I turned to speak to the person standing _____ me.

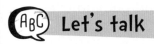 **Let's talk**

Where do you sit in your class? Talk about it.

在課室裏，你的座位是在什麼位置呢？請說一說。

 I sit (e.g. *in front of / on the left of*) _____ .

Let's try 答案： 1. above　2. under　3. behind

Grammar item **85** | **Prepositions of direction**
方向介詞

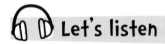

Girl: Oh look, a beautiful butterfly! Oh, it's flown out of the window!

Boy: It's flying toward the tree. Let's go outside to catch it.

Girl: Look! It's flying away from the tree now. Where is it going?

Boy: Come back! Don't fly away! I'll get you and put you into the cage.

Girl: You shouldn't do that. We're not going to hurt any living things.

英文能力 UP！

toward 特別用於美式英語，英式英語通常用 towards。

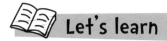 Let's learn

Prepositions of direction tell where to go or where to put something.

方向介詞用來帶出事物移動的方向。

Usage 用法	Examples 例句
away from / toward 離開某處 / 向着 某方向移動	They swam **away from** land. 他們從陸地游出去。
	A bee is flying **toward** us. 一隻蜜蜂向着我們飛過來。
into / out of 進入 / 離開	The little boy jumps **into** the pool. 小男孩跳進泳池裏。
	Don't throw rubbish **out of** the window. 不要把垃圾拋出窗外。
up / down 由下而上 / 由上而下	They are walking **up / down** the stairs. 他們從樓梯走上去 / 走下來。

 Let's try

Fill in the blanks with the correct prepositions.

請在橫線上填上正確的介詞。

1. Let's pour the milk _____ the glass.

2. The firemen quickly climbed _____ the ladders and rescued the little girl.

(ABC) Let's talk

Describe these pictures with the prepositions of direction.

請用方向介詞描述下圖。

1.

2.

Grammar item 86 | Quantifiers - some / any 數量詞

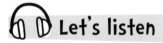 Let's listen

Boy:　I'm really hungry. Let's eat.

Girl:　OK. I've got some yogurt in the fridge, do you want some? I've also got some chocolates in the cupboard, and there're two chicken pies as well.

Boy:　Yea, that sounds great. Do you have any juice?

Girl:　Sure, it's over there. Help yourself.

英文能力 UP！

在對話中，do you want some?（你想要一些嗎？）的 some 並不是數量詞，而是不定代名詞。它不用跟任何名詞連接，能單獨使用。

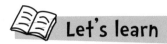 **Let's learn**

We use numbers to represent a count quantity. We use *some* and *any* when we don't know the amount.

如果我們知道確定的數量，就可以用數詞（如 one、two、three）；如果我們不確定數量，就會用 some 和 any。

Usage 用法		Examples 例句
some 一些	**Positives** 肯定句	I want **some** egg rolls. 我想要一些蛋卷。
	Questions 疑問句 **(Answer 答：Yes 是/ 好)**	Do you want **some** juice? 你想要一些果汁嗎？
any 任何	**Negatives** 否定句	I don't want **any** yogurt. 我不想要乳酪。
	Questions 疑問句 **(Answer 答：** **Uncertain 不確定)**	Do you have **any** questions? 你有問題要發問嗎？

注意：any 和 some 可連接可數和不可數名詞（countable nouns and uncountable nouns）。

 **Let's try**

Fill in the blanks with the correct quantifiers.

請在橫線上填上適當的數量詞。

"Do you have 1. _____ sandwiches?"

"No, I don't, but I've got 2. _____ cookies. Do you want some?"

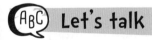 **Let's talk**

Check the fridge and talk about it with your parents.

請檢查冰箱，然後用以下句式跟你父母説一説。

 Is / Are there any _____ (e.g. *milk / soft drinks*)?

 Yes, there is / are some _____ .
No, there isn't / aren't any _____ .

Grammar item **87** | **Quantifiers - much / many / a lot / lots of**
數量詞

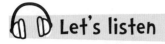 **Let's listen**

Boy: How many people are in the drawing class?

Girl: We don't have many people, just twelve.

Boy: That's great! You can practice a lot. Do you draw many pictures in the class?

Girl: No. I want to draw lots of pictures, but I don't usually have much time to finish the drawing in class. I draw a lot on weekends though.

英文能力 UP！

lots of 是 a lot of 的非正式用法，常在口語中使用。

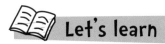 **Let's learn**

These quantifiers are used to describe large amounts.

這些數量詞全都顯示數量「很多」。

Usage 用法			Examples 例句
many	+ countable nouns 可數名詞	Negatives 否定句	He doesn't have **many** friends. 他沒有多少朋友。
		Questions 疑問句	How **many** books have you got? 你有多少本書？
much	+ uncountable nouns 不可數名詞	Negatives 否定句	He doesn't have **much** time. 他沒有多少時間。
		Questions 疑問句	How **much** money have you got? 你有多少錢？
a lot of / lots of	+ countable nouns 可數名詞		He has **a lot of** friends. 他有很多朋友。
	+ uncountable nouns 不可數名詞		He has **a lot of** time. 他有很多時間。

 **Let's try**

Fill in the blanks with the correct quantifiers.

請在橫線上填上適當的數量詞。

"We need to go grocery shopping. We don't have 1. _____

bread or milk, and we don't have 2. _____ drinks."

"No, we've got 3. _____ drinks in the fridge. "

Let's talk

Do you have enough food and drinks at home? Check it out before you go grocery shopping with your parents.

家裏有足夠的食物和飲品嗎？購物前跟你父母一起檢查，然後説一説。

We don't have much / many _____.

Let's try 答案：1. much   2. many   3. lots of / a lot of

187

Grammar item **88** | **Quantifiers - few / little / a few / a little 數量詞**

 Let's listen

Girl: Not everyone is lucky enough to have lots of toys. Some children are very poor. They have few toys to play with and little money to spend. Let's donate to them. How much money have you got?

Boy: I have only a little money left. Just a few dollars.

Girl: I save a little money every month. I can donate more.

Boy: Can I donate other things such as toys or clothes?

英文能力 UP！

a few 和 few、a little 和 little 兩者之間看似相同，只差一個 a 字，但所表示的數量卻差很遠呢！

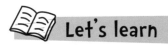 **Let's learn**

little and *few* (without *a*) are negative ideas. *a little* and *a few* are more positive ideas.

a few 和 a little 都是指「一些」，有肯定的意思；few 和 little 則指「幾乎沒有」，有否定的意思。

Usage 用法		Examples 例句
a few 一些	**+ countable nouns** 可數名詞	It will take **a few** minutes. 這需要幾分鐘時間。
few 幾乎沒有		**Few** people knew she was ill. 幾乎沒人知道她病了。
a little 一些	**+ uncountable nouns** 不可數名詞	I have **a little** time to spare. 我還剩下一點空閒時間。
little 幾乎沒有		She has **little** time for him. 她可以花在他身上的時間少得很。

 **Let's try**

Fill in the blanks with the correct quantifiers.

請在橫線上填上適當的數量詞。

1. She drank some tea and ate ＿＿＿＿＿＿ bread.

2. He has ＿＿＿＿＿＿ friends. He is alone all the time.

3. I have lots of homework but very ＿＿＿＿＿＿ time to do it.

 Let's talk

Which playground do you usually go to? What is something that is lacking in it? Talk about it.

你經常去的遊樂場在哪裏？那裏有缺乏什麼設施嗎？請說一說。

> There are ＿＿＿＿＿＿ (e.g. *few slides*) in the playground.

Let's try 答案：1. a little 2. few 3. little

189

Grammar item	**89**	**Quantifiers - none / most / each / all** **數量詞**

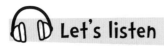 **Let's listen**

Girl: Wow, you have lots of models. Do they all belong to you?

Boy: No, just some of them. Most of them belong to my two cousins, Thomas and Justin. I made none of these model cars. I prefer making model airplanes. Look, this is one of my favorites.

Girl: Brilliant! You have talents I didn't know about.

Boy: Thank you. Thomas, Justin and I are big fans of models. Each of us makes a model every week.

英文能力 UP！

我們用「數量詞 + of」來表示有限數量中的一部分，例如 most of these model cars 指的是「這些模型車中的一大部分」。

190

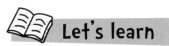 **Let's learn**

We use *all*, *each*, *most*, *none* to talk about quantities, amounts and degree.

我們用 all、each、most、none 來表示不同程度的數量。

Usage 用法	Examples 例句
all (of) 全部、所有	Have you done **all** your homework? 你做完所有功課了嗎？
each (of) 每一	Mr. Smith gave **each of** us a toy. 史密夫先生給我們每人一個玩具。
most (of) 大部分	**Most of** my neighbors are friendly. 我大部分鄰居都很友善。
none (of) 沒有	**None of** these books are mine. 這裏的書沒有一本是我的。

 **Let's try**

Fill in the blanks with the correct quantifiers.

請在橫線上填上適當的數量詞。

1. _____ cars have wheels.

2. _____ of us is reading a different book.

3. _____ of the students passed the exam. It was extremely difficult.

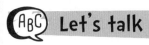 **Let's talk**

Do you and your classmates have the same interests or abilities? Talk about it.

你和同學有共同的興趣或技能嗎？請説一説。

All / each / most / none of my classmates _____ (e.g. *can speak Japanese*).

Grammar item **90** | **To-infinitives**
帶 to 的不定詞

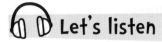 **Let's listen**

Boy: Do you want to go to Wonderland with me? Their new water park has just opened. It has a playground with waterfalls and slides and water animals to ride on.

Girl: Not today. I have a piano exam tomorrow and I need to practice the pieces tonight.

Boy: Oh, I forgot to tell you – the exam is cancelled tomorrow!

Girl: Are you sure?

英文能力 UP！

我們用中文會說「我想去公園」，其中「想」和「去」兩個動詞可以連在一起。但在英文裏，我們不能說 I want go to the park。兩個動詞 want 和 go 必須用 to 連接起來，即 I **want to go** to the park。

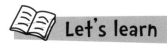

Let's learn

In English, when we want to use two verbs together, we normally put the second verb in the infinitive form.

在英語中，兩個動詞不能隨意連接在一起。有時我們會在兩個動詞之間加上 to，這叫「帶 to 的不定詞」。

Verb A	+ to +	Verb B	Examples 例句
agree			We **agree to go** on a picnic. 我們同意去野餐。
decide			They **decided to leave**. 他們決定離開。
hope	to	原形動詞	She **hopes to study** abroad. 她希望出國留學。
need			I **need to buy** a shirt. 我要買一件恤衫。
want			I **want to speak** to you. 我想跟你説話。

Let's try

Put **to** in the correct position and mark ∧.

請把 to 放在適當的位置，並用 ∧ 標示出來。

> 我們很多時候用帶 to 的不定詞來表示目的或意願。

1. You need clean your room now.

2. She decided buy a doll for her friend.

3. They planned visit America in the summer.

(ABC) Let's talk

What do you need to do in order to be a good boy / girl? Talk about it.

我們應怎樣做一個好孩子呢？請説一説。

> To be a good boy / girl, I need to _____
>
> (e.g. *help out around the house*).

Let's try 答案：1. need to clean　2. decided to buy　3. planned to visit

Grammar item **91** | ## The *-ing* form
-ing 形式

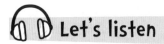 Let's listen

Girl: I miss talking with my best friend. I remember going with her everywhere. Both of us like swimming a lot. We always went shopping together and I enjoyed spending time with her.

Boy: Why did you stop talking?

Girl: She moved to Canada with her family last year.

Boy: I see. I imagine being far apart is difficult.

英文能力 UP！

對話中的一組組動詞不能變成帶 to 的不定詞，例如不能說 I enjoy to spend time with her.（我喜歡跟她在一起。）

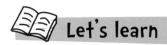 **Let's learn**

For some verbs, when there is another verb following it, we must write the second verb in *-ing* form.

當兩個動詞連在一起，我們有時會把緊接着的第二個動詞改為 -ing 形式。

Verb A	Verb B	Examples 例句
enjoy		He **enjoys playing** the violin. 他喜歡拉小提琴。
finish		I've **finished doing** my homework. 我已經做完功課了。
mind	動詞 **-ing**	Would you **mind waiting** outside? 請你在外面等好嗎？
suggest		She **suggested going** for a walk. 她建議去散步。

 **Let's try**

Fill in the blanks with the correct words.

請根據提示，在橫線上填上正確的答案。

> remember doing 指
> 「記得曾經做過某事」；
> 而 remember to do 指
> 「不要忘記做某事」。

1. I _____ (remember / meet) them at a party once.

2. He _____ (suggest / go) to Wonder Park.

3. What do you _____ (like / do) at the beach?

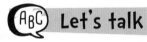 **Let's talk**

What are some things you enjoy doing in your everyday life? Talk about them.

日常生活中有哪些事情你很喜歡做的呢？請説一説。

> I enjoy _____ (e.g. *playing chess with my father*).

Grammar item	92	**Gerunds** 動名詞

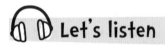

Girl:　Dancing is fun. Let's do some stretching first.

Boy:　I don't like dancing. I'm stiff, and it's hard to follow the moves. And I don't really like wearing ballet suits and performing in front of an audience.

Girl:　What after-class activity have you signed up for then?

Boy:　Cycling. Cycling seems fun.

英文能力 UP！

對話中的 dancing、stretching、cycling 等單詞並不能看作是動詞的現在進行式，它們屬於名詞一類，形容「跳舞」、「伸展」、「騎車」這類活動。

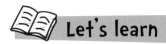

Let's learn

Sometimes, we can put *-ing* at the end of a verb to make it a gerund, which is a type of noun.

有時候，我們會把 -ing 加在動詞後面，令它變成名詞。這類詞語叫「動名詞」，擁有跟名詞一樣的功能，常用來表示活動或動作。

Verb + -ing = Gerund			Examples 例句
read		reading	My hobby is **reading**. 我的嗜好是閱讀。
talk	**+ -ing** ➡	talking	No **talking** in the library! 圖書館裏不准交談！
paint		painting	That **painting** is expensive. 那幅畫很貴。

Let's try

Circle the gerunds in the sentences.

請把句中的動名詞圈出來。

1. She has been doing a lot of shopping.

2. Camping is great fun, but I like jogging more.

3. Anna is good at singing but weak in dancing.

(ABC) Let's talk

Can you tell what these signs mean? Use 'No + gerund' to talk about them.

這些告示代表什麼呢？請用「No + 動名詞」的形式說一說。

1.   2.   3.

Grammar item 93 | Bare infinitives 不帶 to 的不定詞

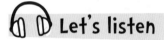 Let's listen

Boy: What's wrong? Why do you look so frightened?

Girl: I heard something drop and break really loud inside the room. I looked into the window but it's too dark to see anything. Then, I heard a man call for help. I also heard a girl cry. That makes me feel so scared.

Boy: Come on, it's actually just the sound of the radio.

Girl: Oh no! How stupid I was. Don't let anybody know about this.

英文能力 UP！

當兩個動詞連在一起的時候，一定要留意第一個動詞是什麼！因為我們以它來決定後面是跟帶 to 或不帶 to 的不定詞，還是使用 -ing 形式。

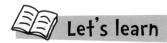

Let's learn

Bare infinitives are usually used after *make* or *let* or other sensory verbs such as *see*, *hear*, *feel*, and *smell*.

我們會在 make、let 或一些感官動詞後面使用不帶 to 的不定詞。

Verb A		Verb B	Examples 例句
make let see hear feel smell	someone or something 某人或物	原形 動詞	I **saw** something **drop** from the balcony. 我看到陽台有東西掉下來。 I **heard** someone **knock** on the door. 我聽到有人在敲門。 Bob **made** Anna **cry** yesterday. 昨天波比把安娜弄哭了。

Let's try

Correct the sentences.

請改正句子，然後填在橫線上。

> 其他連接不帶 to 的不定詞還有 notice、observe、watch 等。

1. Don't let them trying this dangerous game!

_____

2. I felt something wet falls on my face.

_____

Let's talk

Let's play a guessing game. Have your parents put something on your face and move it around. You close your eyes, just feel it and guess what it is.

閉上眼睛，然後請父母把一個物件放在你臉上，讓你猜一猜那是什麼。

I feel something move around my face. Is it _____ (e.g. *a feather*)?

Let's try 答案：1. Don't let them try this dangerous game!
2. I felt something wet fall on my face.

199

Grammar item 94 | Passive voice 被動語態

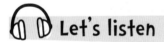 Let's listen

Girl: This picture was drawn by an elephant. Can you believe it?

Boy: That's amazing. Elephants are really clever animals, aren't they?

Girl: Yes, they are. They are trained to perform lots of tasks, such as kicking a ball or carrying people around. Some are even taught to read simple words so that they can communicate with people.

Boy: That's brilliant!

英文能力 UP！

我們説一些被動的事情時，會加上 by 來指出動作是由誰做的。但當我們不清楚做動作的人是誰，便可省略 by 不用。

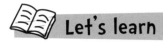

Let's learn

In the active voice, we follow a *subject–verb–object* structure. In the passive voice, the subject receives the action of the verb.

主動語態通常會用「主語＋動詞＋賓語」的結構來說一件事情，被動語態就要把句子的主語和賓語交換身分，用另一方式說相同的事情。

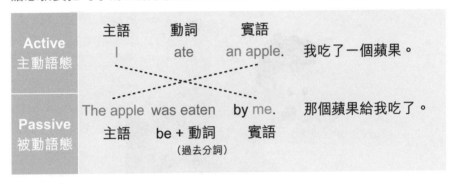

	主語	動詞	賓語	
Active 主動語態	I	ate	an apple.	我吃了一個蘋果。
Passive 被動語態	The apple 主語	was eaten be + 動詞 （過去分詞）	by me. 賓語	那個蘋果給我吃了。

Let's try

Rewrite the sentences in the passive voice.

請用被動語態改寫句子，填在橫線上。

過去分詞一般是由動詞加 -ed 組成，但也有一些不規則變化，請看一看第 220 - 224 頁的附錄。

1. Roger ate the food.

_____

2. Aunt Lily baked these cookies.

_____

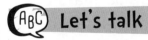

Let's talk

Describe the pictures using the passive voice.

請用被動語態描述下圖，然後說一說。

1.

2.

Let's talk 答案：1. The clothes were folded.　2. The vase was broken.

Let's try 答案：1. The food was eaten by Roger.　2. These cookies were baked by Aunt Lily.

201

Grammar item **95** | **Indirect speech**
間接敍述

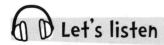 Let's listen

Girl: Where's Perry? Thomas said he bruised his eye!

Boy: He is in his bedroom resting.

Girl: Is he ill?

Boy: He did have a bruise on his eye. He said that he stumbled and fell against the post at the bottom of the stairs. But he said he was alright.

英文能力 UP！

我們轉述別人說話時，會用 said，後面連接 that 和那句話，這叫間接敍述。句中的 that 很多時候都可以刪去，並不影響句子意思。

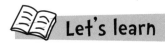 **Let's learn**

When we report the actual words a person said, it is called *direct speech*. When we report what was said, we use *indirect speech*.

「直接敍述」就是用説話者的口吻，把話原原本本地説出來；「間接敍述」就是用另一人的口吻轉述出來。

	Direct speech 直接敍述 用引號一字不漏地引述 別人的話	Indirect speech 間接敍述 轉述別人的話
Rules 規則	① The first person 第一人稱 ② Verb 動詞	The third person 第三人稱 Past Simple 簡單過去式
Examples 例句	She said, "I am happy." 她説：「我很開心。」	She said that she was happy. 她説她很開心。
	He said, "I have passed the exam." 他説：「我通過了考試。」	He said that he had passed the exam. 他説他通過了考試。

 **Let's try**

Rewrite the sentences in indirect speech.

請把句子改寫成間接敍述句，填在橫線上。

1. "I want to be a scientist," said George.

_____

2. Uncle Pang said, "I have bought you a present."

_____

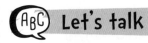 **Let's talk**

Repeat what your mother said in indirect speech.

請用間接敍述的方式重複媽媽説的話。

 | I love you. | Mom said she loved me. |

Let's try 答案： 1. George said (that) he wanted to be a scientist.
2. Uncle Pang said (that) he had bought me a present.

Grammar item 96 | Types of sentences
句子的類型

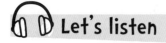 **Let's listen**

Boy: Look! The rubbish bin is on fire! Oh, what should we do?
        感歎句   疑問句
        Fire! Fire! Help! Help!

Girl: Be calm! Be quiet!

Boy: Fetch some buckets of water! Quick! Let's pour water on
        祈使句
        it.

Girl: No, that's very dangerous. Come with me. We can ask an
        adult for help. We can also call up the Fire Department.
                                                    陳述句

英文能力 UP！

對話中使用了英文中四種不同的句型，理解這些句型，對我們理解句
子、使用標點、表達感情等都會大有好處。

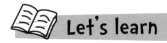

Let's learn

There are four main types of sentences and each creates a different mood through the speaker's tone.

我們可根據説話的語氣和句子的結構，把句子分為四種類型。

Types 種類	Functions 用途	Examples 例句	Puntuation 句末標點
Statement 陳述句	Express a fact 説明事實	The sun rises in the east. 太陽從東方升起。	Period (.)
Question 疑問句	Ask a question 發問	How hot is the sun? 太陽有多熱？	Question mark (?)
Command 祈使句	Give a command / make a request 發出指令或請求	Be quiet! 安靜點！	Exclamation mark (!) / Period (.)
Exclamation 感歎句	Express great emotion 抒發強烈感情	What a lovely day! 多好的天氣啊！	Exclamation mark (!) / Period (.)

Let's try

Draw lines to pair up in groups.

請辨別以下句子的句型，然後用線連起來。

1. Exclamation •   • A. Don't swim in the river!

2. Command •   • B. What awful weather!

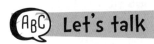

Let's talk

Imagine you are this whale. What would you say?

假設你是這條鯨魚，你會説什麼？請用不同的句型説一説。

There's so much rubbish in the ocean.

Grammar item 97 | 5W1H Questions 六何疑問句

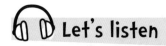

Boy: What's that?

Girl: I got a birthday invitation from Thomas.

Boy: **Where** is he going to have the party? **When** will it be? **How** many friends has he invited? **Whom** has he invited? **What** present are you going to buy for him?

Girl: Hey, would you stop asking so many questions?

英文能力 UP！

有些疑問句只需要回答 Yes 或 No，而六何疑問句（who 何人？、when 何時？、where 何地？、what 何事？、why 為何？、how 如何？）則要求我們針對問題而回答具體的資料。

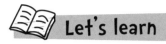 **Let's learn**

The 5W1H questions are used to ask for information about an event or situation.

六何疑問句可用來發問有關某事情或情況的各種資料。

		Examples 例句
5W	**Who?** 何人	**Who** is Michael? 誰是米高？
	When? 何時	**When** is his birthday? 他什麼時候生日？
	Where? 何地	**Where** does he live? 他住在哪裏？
	What? 何事 / 什麼	**What** are his hobbies? 他有什麼嗜好？
	Why? 為何	**Why** does he always wear a cap? 他為何總是戴着帽子？
1H	**How?** 如何	**How** did you meet? 你們是怎樣認識的？

 **Let's try**

Write questions about the colored words.

請根據着色文字的提示，把句子改寫成疑問句，填在橫線上。

1. Question: _____
   Answer: I go to school on foot.

2. Question:_____
   Answer: She drank tea.

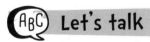 **Let's talk**

Ask your parents to think about a relative or friend. Then you ask questions to guess who he / she has in mind. Keep asking 5W1H questions to narrow down the possibilities until you can guess the exact answer.

請你父母想出一個親友，然後你用六何疑問句發問，直至猜出那是誰。

Guess who I'm thinking about?

Let's try 答案：1. How do you go to school?　2. What did she drink?

Grammar item 98 | Question tags 附加問句

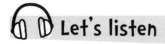 Let's listen

Girl: You're going out, aren't you?

Boy: Yep. It's such a nice day today, isn't it? It'd be a shame to stay indoors.

Girl: Yes, we should do something. What do you have in mind?

Boy: I'm going to fly a kite. You're coming with me, aren't you?

Girl: Okay.

英文能力 UP!

回答附加問句時，無論問題是如何提問，只要事實是肯定的，就用 yes；如事實是否定的，就用 no。

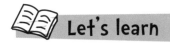 **Let's learn**

We use question tags to ask for a confirmation.

我們説完主要的句子後，再加上一個短問句，看看對方是不是同意自己的看法，這種短問句叫附加問句。

Rule 規則 ①	**Positive statement + Negative question tag** 陳述句用肯定動詞，附加問句就要用否定動詞
Examples 例句	It's raining, **isn't it? / is it not?** 現在在下雨，不是嗎？ Anna has gone home, **hasn't she? / has she not?** 安娜已回家了，不是嗎？
Rule 規則 ②	**Negative statement + Positive question tag** 陳述句用否定動詞，附加問句就要用肯定動詞
Examples 例句	David can't swim, **can he?** 大衞不會游泳，是嗎？ You aren't going out, **are you?** 你不準備外出，是嗎？

 **Let's try**

Fill in the blanks with suitable question tags.

請在橫線上填上正確的附加問句。

主要句子和附加問句之間，要用逗號分隔開啊！

1. We must hurry, _____ ?

2. Your father is a doctor, _____ ?

3. Irina can play the violin well, _____ ?

 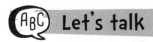 **Let's talk**

Learn these weather greetings. Practice them.

美國人習慣用天氣作為開場白，請根據今天的天氣跟別人打個招呼吧。

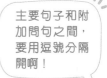

It's a nice / beautiful day, isn't it?
The weather is terrible today, isn't it?

209

Let's try 答案：1. mustn't we　2. isn't he　3. can't she

Grammar item **99** | **First conditional**
第一條件句

 Let's listen

胃部不適

Boy: I don't feel well today. I have an upset stomach. Maybe I had too much cold food.

Girl: If you feel sick, go to the doctor.

Boy: I don't want to go to the doctor. If I go to the doctor, I'll have to take medicine or get a shot. I think I'll feel better if I take a rest and get some sleep.

Girl: Are you sure? If you don't go to the doctor, you will be sicker!

英文能力UP！

對話中的 If you feel sick, go to the doctor! 是一個結合了祈使句的條件句，意思是：如果你感覺不舒服，就要去看醫生！

210

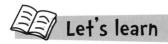 **Let's learn**

The first conditional talks about something that is likely to happen.

第一條件句用來說明必然會發生的情況或結果。很多條件句都用上 if 這個單詞,來顯示「如果出現 A 條件,就會產生 B 結果」的意思。

Rule 規則 ①	If + condition (Present simple), 條件(簡單現在式)		result (Future simple) 結果(簡單將來式)
Examples **例句**	**If** 如果	you don't work hard 你不用功	you **will** fail. 你便會失敗。
	If 如果	it rains 下雨	we **will** stay at home. 我們會留在家裏。
Rule 規則 ②	Result (Future simple) + if + condition (Present simple) 結果(簡單將來式)　　　　　條件(簡單現在式)		
Example 例句	They **will not** be late **if** they leave now. 如果他們現在離開就不會遲到了。		

 **Let's try**

Fill in the blanks with the correct words.

請在橫線上填上正確的答案。

1. _____ you scream, someone will hear us.

2. If you don't hurry, you _____ _____ the train.

3. They _____ _____ swimming _____ it's a sunny day.

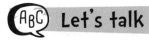 **Let's talk**

What will you do if you have three hundred dollars? Talk about it.

假設你有三百元,你會做些什麼呢?請說一說。

If I have three hundred dollars, I will _____.

Grammar item **100** | **Second conditional**
第二條件句

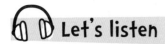 **Let's listen**

Boy: Do you ever wish you could travel in time?

Girl: No, but I wish I could have wings. If I had wings, I could fly like a bird. If I were a bird, I could fly to the top of a tree. I could fly to the top of a mountain. I could even fly to the moon.

Boy: I'd rather fly on a broomstick. That would look very cool!

英文能力 UP！

If I were a bird（如果我是一隻鳥）中，為什麼是用 were 而不是用 am 或 was 呢？這是英語裏的一個特別用法，當現實與願望不一致時，就會用上這種句式。

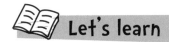 **Let's learn**

The second conditional is used to talk about unlikely or impossible situations.

第二條件句帶有假設語氣，用來説明不大可能發生的情況。

Rule 規則 ①	If + condition (Past simple), result (would / could + verb) 假設情況（簡單過去式）　結果（**would / could** + 動詞)		
Examples 例句	**If** 如果	I had wings 我有一雙翅膀	**I could** fly. 我就能飛。
	If 如果	I were you 我是你的話	**I would not** do that. 我就不會那樣做。
Rule 規則 ②	**I wish I** + condition (Past simple) 假設情況（簡單過去式）		
Example 例句	**I wish I** 但願我	**could** fly. 能飛。	

 **Let's try**

Circle the correct answers.

請把正確的答案圈出來。

1. I wish I (could sing / can sing / sang) better.

2. If you (have / has / had) longer legs, you would run faster.

3. If you could travel anywhere in the world, where (will / can / would) you go?

 Let's talk

What would you wish for if you ever saw a shooting star? Talk about it.

如果看到流星，你會許下什麼願望呢？請説一説。

> 記住用簡單過去式來講出你的願望啊。

I wish I _____.

Let's Play 1

可在學習
Section 1 時，
完成這練習。

Fill in the crossword puzzle with the correct plural nouns of the following list.

請根據提示，填上正確的複數名詞。如沒有複數，
請直接填上該名詞。

	Down	A foot	B ox	C child	D air
		E cattle	F sheep		
	Across	1 mouse	2 tea	3 person	4 lorry
		5 woman	6 water	7 tooth	

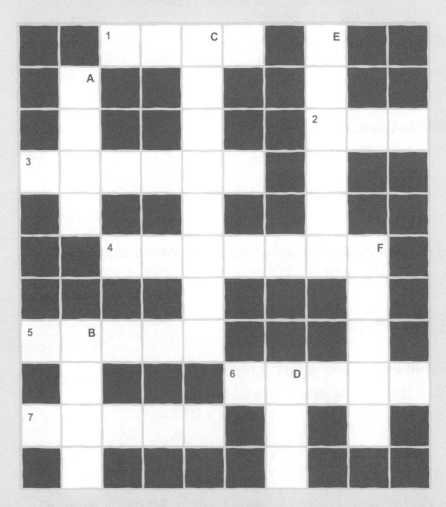

214

Let's Play 2

可在學習 Section 4 和 5 時，完成這練習。

Fill in the crossword puzzle with the past tense of the following verbs.

請根據提示，填上正確的動詞過去式。

| **Down** | **A** spit | **B** blow | **C** rise | **D** understand |
| | **E** give | **F** win | **G** fall | |

| **Across** | **1** find | **2** see | **3** dig | **4** eat |
| | **5** tell | **6** write | **7** ride | **8** drink |

Let's Play 3

可在學習 Section 4 和 5 時，完成這 練習。

Fill in the crossword puzzle with the past participles of the following verbs.
請根據提示，填上正確的過去分詞。

Down	A leave	B keep	C break	
	D lead	E bring	F catch	
Across	1 kneel	2 draw	3 begin	4 forget
	5 grow	6 make	7 tell	

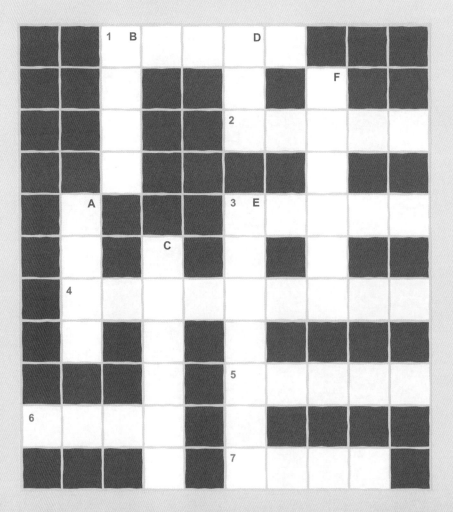

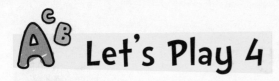

Let's Play 4

可在學習
Section 9 時，
完成這練習。

Fill in the crossword puzzle with the correct conjunctions.
請根據提示，填上正確的連接詞。

Down

A I go to bed _____ I've taken a shower.

B You can have _____ milk or juice.

C We waited _____ the rain stopped.

D Dad was thin _____ he was young.

Across

1 _____ he was ill, he went to school.

2 They are poor _____ happy.

3 Do you want salad _____ ice cream?

4 I won't talk to you _____ you say sorry.

Let's Play 5

可在學習
Section 10 時，
完成這練習。

Fill in the crossword puzzle with the opposites of the following adverbs.

請根據提示，填上意思相反或相對的副詞。

| Down | A here | B loudly | C out |
| | D yesterday | E poorly | F back |

| Across | 1 downstairs | 2 hardly |
| | 3 slightly | 4 quickly |

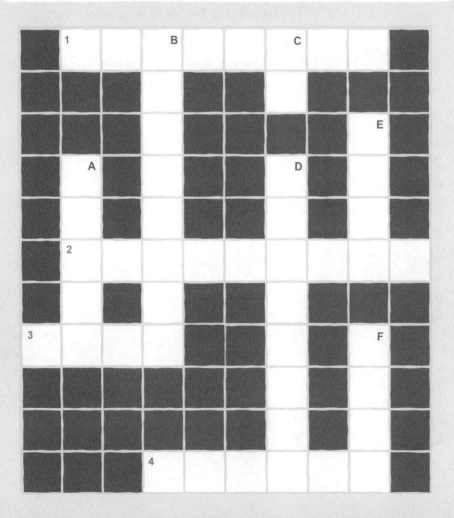

218

Answer key 答案

Let's Play 1

Let's Play 4

Let's Play 2

Let's Play 5

Let's Play 3

Irregular verbs 不規則動詞

✿ 這個表格包含小學階段常用的 135 個不規則動詞。

✿ 簡單現在式一欄中，括號內的動詞表示與 he、she、it 或其他
  單數名詞連用時的變化。

✿ 限於篇幅，每個動詞只列出一個中文解釋。

Present simple 簡單現在式	Present participle 現在分詞	Past simple 簡單過去式	Past participle 過去分詞
advise (advises) 勸告	advising	advised	advised
agree (agrees) 同意	agreeing	agreed	agreed
apologize (apologizes) 道歉	apologizing	apologized	apologized
argue (argues) 爭論	arguing	argued	argued
arrange (arranges) 安排	arranging	arranged	arranged
arrive (arrives) 到達	arriving	arrived	arrived
bake (bakes) 烤	baking	baked	baked
be (am / is / are) 是	being	was / were	been
become (becomes) 變成	becoming	became	become
begin (begins) 開始	beginning	began	begun
believe (believes) 相信	believing	believed	believed
bite (bites) 咬	biting	bit	bitten
blame (blames) 責備	blaming	blamed	blamed
bleed (bleeds) 流血	bleeding	bled	bled
blow (blows) 吹	blowing	blew	blown
break (breaks) 打破	breaking	broke	broken
breathe (breathes) 呼吸	breathing	breathed	breathed
bring (brings) 帶來	bringing	brought	brought
build (builds) 建築	building	built	built
buy (buys) 購買	buying	bought	bought
catch (catches) 捕捉	catching	caught	caught
chat (chats) 閒談	chatting	chatted	chatted

Present simple 簡單現在式	Present participle 現在分詞	Past simple 簡單過去式	Past participle 過去分詞
choose (chooses) 選擇	choosing	chose	chosen
clap (claps) 拍手	clapping	clapped	clapped
close (closes) 關閉	closing	closed	closed
come (comes) 來	coming	came	come
cry (cries) 哭泣	crying	cried	cried
cut (cuts) 切	cutting	cut	cut
cycle (cycles) 騎自行車	cycling	cycled	cycled
damage (damages) 破壞	damaging	damaged	damaged
decide (decides) 決定	deciding	decided	decided
dig (digs) 挖	digging	dug	dug
do (does) 做	doing	did	done
donate (donates) 捐贈	donating	donated	donated
draw (draws) 繪畫	drawing	drew	drawn
dream (dreams) 做夢	dreaming	dreamed / dreamt	dreamed / dreamt
drink (drinks) 喝	drinking	drank	drunk
drive (drives) 駕駛	driving	drove	driven
eat (eats) 吃	eating	ate	eaten
exercise (exercises) 做運動	exercising	exercised	exercised
fall (falls) 跌倒	falling	fell	fallen
feed (feeds) 餵飼	feeding	fed	fed
feel (feels) 感覺	feeling	felt	felt
fight (fights) 打架	fighting	fought	fought
find (finds) 尋找	finding	found	found
fly (flies) 飛	flying	flew	flown
forget (forgets) 忘記	forgetting	forgot	forgotten
forgive (forgives) 原諒	forgiving	forgave	forgiven

Present simple 簡單現在式	Present participle 現在分詞	Past simple 簡單過去式	Past participle 過去分詞
get (gets) 取得	getting	got	gotten / got
give (gives) 給予	giving	gave	given
go (goes) 去	going	went	gone
grow (grows) 生長	growing	grew	grown
guess (guesses) 猜測	guessing	guessed	guessed
hang (hangs) 掛	hanging	hung / hanged	hung / hanged
hate (hates) 憎恨	hating	hated	hated
have (has) 有	having	had	had
hear (hears) 聽	hearing	heard	heard
hide (hides) 躲藏	hiding	hid	hidden
hit (hits) 打	hitting	hit	hit
hold (holds) 拿住	holding	held	held
hope (hopes) 希望	hoping	hoped	hoped
hug (hugs) 擁抱	hugging	hugged	hugged
hurt (hurts) 弄傷	hurting	hurt	hurt
imagine (imagines) 想像	imagining	imagined	imagined
invite (invites) 邀請	inviting	invited	invited
jog (jogs) 慢跑	jogging	jogged	jogged
keep (keeps) 保留	keeping	kept	kept
kneel (kneels) 跪下	kneeling	knelt / kneeled	knelt / kneeled
know (knows) 知道	knowing	knew	known
learn (learns) 學習	learning	learned / learnt	learned / learnt
leave (leaves) 離開	leaving	left	left
lend (lends) 借出	lending	lent	lent
let (lets) 讓	letting	let	let
lie (lies) 說謊	lying	lied	lied
lie (down) (lies) 躺下	lying (down)	lay	lain
light (lights) 點火	lighting	lit / lighted	lit / lighted
like (likes) 喜歡	liking	liked	liked

Present simple 簡單現在式	Present participle 現在分詞	Past simple 簡單過去式	Past participle 過去分詞
lose (loses) 遺失	losing	lost	lost
love (loves) 愛	loving	loved	loved
make (makes) 做	making	made	made
meet (meets) 見面	meeting	met	met
pay (pays) 付款	paying	paid	paid
plan (plans) 計劃	planning	planned	planned
prepare (prepares) 準備	preparing	prepared	prepared
put (puts) 放	putting	put	put
quarrel (quarrels) 爭吵	quarrelling	quarrelled	quarrelled
read (reads) 閱讀	reading	read	read
reply (replies) 回答	replying	replied	replied
ride (rides) 騎	riding	rode	ridden
ring (rings) 響起	ringing	rang	rung
rise (rises) 上升	rising	rose	risen
rub (rubs) 擦	rubbing	rubbed	rubbed
run (runs) 跑	running	ran	run
saw (saws) 鋸	sawing	sawed	sawn
say (says) 説	saying	said	said
see (sees) 看見	seeing	saw	seen
sell (sells) 賣	selling	sold	sold
send (sends) 寄出	sending	sent	sent
shake (shakes) 搖動	shaking	shook	shaken
shoot (shoots) 射擊	shooting	shot	shot
shop (shops) 購物	shopping	shopped	shopped
show (shows) 展示	showing	showed	shown
shut (shuts) 關閉	shutting	shut	shut
sing (sings) 唱歌	singing	sang	sung
sink (sinks) 下沉	sinking	sank	sunk
sit (sits) 坐	sitting	sat	sat

Present simple 簡單現在式	Present participle 現在分詞	Past simple 簡單過去式	Past participle 過去分詞
sleep (sleeps) 睡覺	sleeping	slept	slept
slide (slides) 滑行	sliding	slid	slid
smell (smells) 嗅	smelling	smelt / smelled	smelt / smelled
smile (smiles) 微笑	smiling	smiled	smiled
spit (spits) 吐痰	spitting	spat	spat
speak (speaks) 說話	speaking	spoke	spoken
spend (spends) 花費	spending	spent	spent
spell (spells) 拼寫	spelling	spelt / spelled	spelt / spelled
spill (spills) 溢出	spilling	spilt / spilled	spilt / spilled
stand (stands) 站立	standing	stood	stood
steal (steals) 偷	stealing	stole	stolen
sweep (sweeps) 打掃	sweeping	swept	swept
swim (swims) 游泳	swimming	swam	swum
take (takes) 拿着	taking	took	taken
teach (teaches) 教	teaching	taught	taught
tease (teases) 取笑	teasing	teased	teased
tell (tells) 告訴	telling	told	told
think (thinks) 認為	thinking	thought	thought
throw (throws) 拋	throwing	threw	thrown
tidy (tidies) 整理	tidying	tidied	tidied
try (tries) 嘗試	trying	tried	tried
understand (understands) 明白	understanding	understood	understood
use (uses) 用	using	used	used
wake (wakes) 醒來	waking	woke	woken
wear (wears) 穿	wearing	wore	worn
win (wins) 贏	winning	won	won
wish (wishes) 期望	wishing	wished	wished
worry (worries) 擔心	worrying	worried	worried
write (writes) 寫	writing	wrote	written

Numbers 數字

0	zero
1	one
2	two
3	three
4	four
5	five
6	six
7	seven
8	eight
9	nine
10	ten
11	eleven
12	twelve
13	thirteen
14	fourteen
15	fifteen
16	sixteen
17	seventeen
18	eighteen
19	nineteen

20	twenty
21	twenty-one
22	twenty-two
23	twenty-three
24	twenty-four
25	twenty-five
26	twenty-six
27	twenty-seven
28	twenty-eight
29	twenty-nine
30	thirty
40	forty
50	fifty
60	sixty
70	seventy
80	eighty
90	ninety

Large numbers 較大的數

100	one hundred
101	one hundred and one
200	two hundred
300	three hundred
400	four hundred
500	five hundred
600	six hundred
700	seven hundred
800	eight hundred
900	nine hundred
1,000	one thousand
2,000	two thousand
10,000	ten thousand
100,000	one hundred thousand
1,000,000	one million
10,000,000	ten million

123,456,789

One hundred and twenty-three million, four hundred and fifty-six thousand, seven hundred and eighty nine

Ordinal numbers 序數

1 st	first	11 th	eleventh
2 nd	second	12 th	twelfth
3 rd	third	13 th	thirteenth
4 th	fourth	14 th	fourteenth
5 th	fifth	15 th	fifteenth
6 th	sixth	16 th	sixteenth
7 th	seventh	17 th	seventeenth
8 th	eighth	18 th	eighteenth
9 th	ninth	19 th	nineteenth
10 th	tenth	20 th	twentieth

21 st	twenty-first
22 nd	twenty-second
23 rd	twenty-third
24 th	twenty-fourth
25 th	twenty-fifth
26 th	twenty-sixth
27 th	twenty-seventh
28 th	twenty-eighth
29 th	twenty-ninth
30 th	thirtieth

Uses of ordinal numbers 序數的用法

Dates	日期	His birthday is on May 20 th .
Centuries	世紀	Mozart was born in the 18 th century.
Sequence	次序	Angela came second in the race.
Floors of a building	樓層	The restaurant is on the 5 th floor.

Time 時間

Units of time
時間單位

1 second 秒

1 minute 分鐘 = 60 seconds

1 hour 小時 = 60 minutes

1 day 日 = 24 hours

1 week 周 = 7 days

1 fortnight 兩周 = 2 weeks

1 month 月 = 28 - 31 days

1 year 年 = 12 months

1 decade 十年 = 10 years

1 century 世紀 = 100 years

Times of the day
一天裏的時間

dawn — 黎明；破曉

morning — 上午；早上

noon / midday — 中午；正午

afternoon — 下午

dusk — 黃昏

evening — 傍晚；晚上（日落至睡覺前）

night — 夜晚（日落至次日日出）

midnight — 午夜

❶ It's ... o'clock.

❷ It's five past ...

❸ It's ten past ...

❹ It's a quarter past ...

❺ It's twenty past ...

❻ It's twenty-five past ...

❼ It's half past ...

❽ It's twenty-five to ...

❾ It's twenty to ...

❿ It's a quarter to ...

⓫ It's ten to ...

⓬ It's five to ...

注意： 美國孩子常常把 past 說成 after，例如 a quarter after five（5:15）。他們又會把 to 說成 till，例如 a quarter till nine（8:45）。

Days, months, seasons
日、月、季節

Days of the week 星期

Sunday 星期日	
Monday 星期一	
Tuesday 星期二	
Wednesday 星期三	
Thursday 星期四	
Friday 星期五	
Saturday 星期六	

Months of the year 月份

January 一月	July 七月
February 二月	August 八月
March 三月	September 九月
April 四月	October 十月
May 五月	November 十一月
June 六月	December 十二月

Seasons 季節

Spring 春天

Fall 秋天

Summer 夏天

Winter 冬天

Countable and uncountable nouns
可數與不可數名詞

Countable food 可數的食物

sandwich 三明治

apple 蘋果

pear 梨

hamburger 漢堡包

salad 沙律

vegetable 蔬菜

potato 馬鈴薯

tomato 番茄

carrot 蘿蔔

onion 洋蔥

watermelon 西瓜

eggplant 茄子

Uncountable food 不可數的食物

bread 麵包

rice 米飯

pasta 意大利麵

flour 麵粉

meat 肉

jam 果醬

jelly 果凍

butter 牛油

soup 湯

tea 茶

juice 果汁

milk 牛奶

Collective nouns 集合名詞

Grammar Handbook
文法手帳

Animals 動物

a flock of geese
一羣鵝

a litter of puppies
一窩小狗

a school of fish
一羣魚

a troop of lions
一羣獅子

a swarm of bees
一羣蜜蜂

a nest of mice
一窩老鼠

a flight of swallows
一羣飛燕

a pack of wolves
一羣狼

a herd of cattle
一羣牛

an army of ants
一羣螞蟻

People 人物

a band of musicians
一隊樂隊

a crew of sailors
一組船員

a class of pupils
一班學生

a gang of criminals
一幫匪徒

a team of workers
一組工人

Food quantifiers 食物量詞

Grammar Handbook
文法手帳

a bag of potato chips
一袋薯片

a loaf of baguette
一條麵包

a slice of pizza
一片薄餅

a bottle of water
一瓶水

an ear of corn
一條粟米

a scoop of ice cream
一勺冰淇淋

a basket of fruit
一籃水果

a carton of eggs
一盒雞蛋

a pot of tea
一壺茶

a bar of chocolate
一排巧克力

a can of Coke
一罐可樂

a piece of cake
一件蛋糕

a bucket of popcorn
一桶爆谷

a bunch of bananas
一串香蕉

a packet of biscuits
一包餅乾

Action verbs 動態動詞

catch 接住

climb 爬

kick 踢

lean 斜靠

pull 拉

push 推

crawl 爬行

lie 躺臥

fall 跌倒

lift 抬起

slip 滑倒

jump 跳

pick up 拾起

skip 跳繩

wave 揮手

Adjectives 形容詞

An adjective is used to describe a noun or pronoun. It can tell us many things, such as:

形容詞用來描述名詞或代名詞，讓我們了解那些名詞或代名詞究竟是怎麼樣的，例如：

Opinion 意見	Size & Age 尺寸 / 年歲	Shape 形狀
beautiful 漂亮	small / big 小 / 大	round 圓形的
ugly 醜陋	tall / short 高 / 矮	square 方形的
delicious 美味	young / old 年輕 / 年老	rectangular 長方形的
boring 沉悶	new / old 新 / 舊	triangular 三角形的

Feel 觸覺	Sound 聲音	Weather 天氣
hard 堅硬	loud 嘈吵	sunny 晴天的
smooth 滑溜	soft 柔和	cloudy 陰天的
soft 柔軟	weak 微弱	rainy 雨天的
rough 粗糙	sharp 尖銳	windy 颳風的

Emotions 情緒	Color 顏色	Smell 氣味
happy 開心	red 紅色	pleasant 芬芳的
angry 生氣	purple 紫色	nasty 難聞的
nervous 緊張	black 黑色	fishy 腥臭的
		acidic 酸的

Taste 味道
sweet 甜的
bitter 苦的
sour 酸的
spicy 辣的

Material 材料
wooden 木製的
plastic 塑料製的
cotton 棉質的

Origin 國籍 / 產地
American 美國（製）的
British 英國（製）的
Japanese 日本（製）的

near / next to

in

on

off

behind

below

into

in front of

above

onto

out of

opposite

between

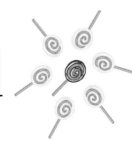

around

代名詞	第一人稱 單數	第一人稱 複數	第二人稱 單數	第二人稱 複數	第三人稱 單數	第三人稱 單數	第三人稱 單數	第三人稱 複數
主格	I 我	we 我們	you 你	you 你們	he 他	she 她	it 它／牠	they 他們
賓格	me 我	us 我們	you 你	you 你們	him 他	her 她	it 它／牠	them 他們
所有格	my 我的	our 我們的	your 你的	your 你們的	his 他的	her 她的	its 它／牠的	their 他們的
物主	mine 我的	ours 我們的	yours 你的	yours 你們的	his 他的	hers 她的	its 它／牠的	theirs 他們的
反身	myself 我自己	ourselves 我們自己	yourself 你自己	yourselves 你們自己	himself 他自己	herself 她自己	itself 它／牠自己	themselves 他們自己

Quantifiers 量詞

Quantifiers

With uncountable nouns 連接不可數名詞

- much 很多
- a little / little / very little 一些 / 幾乎沒有
- a bit of 一點
- a great deal of 大量
- a large quantity of 大量
- a large amount of 大量

With countable nouns 連接可數名詞

- many 很多
- several 幾個
- a few / few / very few 一些 / 幾乎沒有
- a great / large number of 大量
- a number of 一些
- a majority of 大部分

With countable and uncountable nouns 連接可數或不可數名詞

- enough 足夠的
- all 全部所有
- more 更多 / most 大部分
- less 更少 / least 最少
- no / none 沒有
- a lot of 大量
- lots of 大量
- plenty of 大量
- some 一些
- any 任何

I have lots of toys.

Punctuation 標點符號

Grammar Handbook 文法手帳

:	**Colon** 冒號 A colon is used before giving examples. 用來引出下文各項 I like all kinds of fruit : apples, pears, oranges, etc.
;	**Semi-colon** 分號 A semi-colon is used to separate parts of a sentence. 用來分隔句子中的不同部分 This school bag is expensive; that one is cheap.
( )	**Brackets** 括號 Brackets are used to separate extra information from the main sentence or statement. 用來分隔句子中額外的信息 One of the winners (Thomas) is my friend.
-	**Hyphen** 連字號 A hyphen is used to join two or more words to form a new word. 用來把兩個或以上的單詞組合成為一個單詞 thirty - three
—	**Dash** 破折號 A dash is used to give extra information. 用於補充說明 What do you want — A, B, or C?

.	**Period** 句號（英：Full stop) A full stop marks the end of a sentence. 用於表示句子完結 I like reading .
?	**Question mark** 問號 A question mark is used at the end of a question. 用於問句末尾 Where is my school bag ?
!	**Exclamation mark** 感歎號 An exclamation mark is used when you are excited, angry, or surprised about something. 用於表示興奮、憤怒、驚訝等強烈感情 Be careful !
" "	**Quotation marks** 引號 Quotation marks are used to show what someone said or wrote. 用於直接引用語句 " What is this ? " he asked.
,	**Comma** 逗號 A comma is used to show a short stop in a sentence. 用在句子中表示稍作停頓 I felt bored , tired , and sleepy.